DARROW'S WORD

It might have been Christmas in Wyoming but there certainly was no good cheer for Sheriff Darrow, for he had a cold-blooded murder to contend with. Worse still, it looked as if the charming Beatrix Verstappen could be the guilty party. Certainly she was the only witness, so Darrow slammed her into jail. But that didn't go down well with the town's menfolk. Beatrix's brother, Henk, vowed to free her and, as blizzards isolated the town, he made his desperate plans . . .

D1609827

GILLIAN F. TAYLOR

DARROW'S WORD

Complete and Unabridged

LINFORD
Leicester

First published in Great Britain in 2001 by
Robert Hale Limited
London

First Linford Edition
published 2002
by arrangement with
Robert Hale Limited
London

British Library CIP Data

Taylor, Gillian F.
    Darrow's word.—Large print ed.—
Linford western library
    1. Western stories
    2. Large type books
    I. Title
    823.9′14 [F]

    ISBN 0–7089–9903–4

Published by
F. A. Thorpe (Publishing)
Anstey, Leicestershire

Set by Words & Graphics Ltd.
Anstey, Leicestershire
Printed and bound in Great Britain by
T. J. International Ltd., Padstow, Cornwall

This book is printed on acid-free paper

1

Hugh Keating shivered miserably and hunched his shoulders inside his grey overcoat as he hurried along the sidewalk. His breath clouded around his face as he thought longingly of log fires, deep rugs, hot tea, and crumpets with butter and jam. None of those luxuries was available to him in Govan, the little Wyoming town where he now lived and reluctantly worked. Hugh made his way along Cross Street, glowering at the piles of frozen snow that lingered among the slush. He was supposed to be doing the rounds of the town in his capacity as deputy sheriff, but he was seriously considering whether to nip into the Freight Car saloon for half an hour.

It was still mid-afternoon, but this close to Christmas the day was already gloomy and few other people were out. Hugh Keating paused to peer at the window of Miss McKenna's fancy goods store. He stared at the tortoiseshell-backed brush-and-comb set and wondered whether it was a suitable gift for Minnie Davis. He didn't notice the horse and rider on the quiet street until an impatient voice broke into his thoughts.

'Oh, get on with you, you stubborn beast!'

A young woman was riding side-saddle on a dainty roan mare which had stopped in front of a large puddle of dirty slush. 'Go on!' the rider insisted, hitting the mare hard with her whip. The roan mare laid back her ears and poked her nose in the air. The angry rider shouted and struck her again, causing the horse to back up and roll her eyes.

Hugh Keating had never been much of a horseman but even he could tell that the mare's anxiety about the puddle was fast turning to fear. He jumped off the sidewalk and approached carefully.

'Miss Verstappen? May I help?'

The young woman noticed him for the first time and stopped hitting her horse. After a moment's pause, she smiled widely at him.

'Deputy Keating. How nice to see you.'

Hugh stood up straighter and smiled foolishly in return. He was always delighted when a woman smiled at him, especially when it was one as enchanting as Miss Beatrix Verstappen. She was a pretty doll of a young woman, barely five feet tall and dainty in everything from her fashionable clothes to the curls of her dusky blonde hair. The cold weather had brought a becoming blush of colour to her peachy skin and added sparkle to her green eyes. Hugh was particularly pleased that she didn't address him as 'lord', as every other American seemed to do; it never failed to irritate him.

'Is that a new horse?' Hugh asked. His time in the West hadn't altered his cultured English accent in the slightest, which was what attracted the nickname he hated.

'Yes. My brother, Henk, had her sent out specially from Kentucky for me,' Beatrix Verstappen said. 'I called her 'Paris', because she's so fashionable and pretty.'

'But Paris was male,' said Hugh, who had scraped through a classical education at Harrow and Cambridge, and was thinking of the Trojan War.

Beatrix frowned. She knew nothing of the classics and suspected that he was making fun of her. Hugh saw her expression and hastened to make amends.

'She's a lovely horse,' he said. 'I think she's just nervous of new surroundings perhaps.'

'I expect you're right.' Beatrix knew exactly how to twist men around her little finger and Hugh's admiring looks had shown her an easy target. Men who were half in love with her never teased her. 'I'm sure you're much better with

4

horses than I am.'

'Would you like me to lead her through the puddle?' Hugh offered.

'How gallant!' Beatrix exclaimed, making Hugh swell with pride. 'It would be such a help,' she went on as he took the reins and led the mare down the street. 'I think I'm late already and I've still got to take her to the livery barn.'

'Where are you going?' Hugh asked, manfully striding through slushy puddles without complaint as long as Beatrix was talking to him.

'To the Wells, Fargo office. I promised Mother I wouldn't be out long but Paris has been shying and fooling around so much, I've got all behind.' As they talked, they had reached the crossroads at the centre of Govan. There were only two real roads in town, Main Street and Cross Street, with a maze of alleys between the buildings scattered around those fixed routes. The livery barn was at the north end of Main Street and the Wells, Fargo office was down at the south end, near the railway depot.

'I could see to the horse for you,' Hugh offered.

'Would you really? That would be a wonderful help.' Beatrix allowed Hugh to help her from the side-saddle. She flashed her brilliant smile up at him, making him feel uncommonly tall and masculine. 'I'm so grateful to you, Deputy Keating.'

'Call me Hugh.'

She smiled again, and was running along the sidewalk past the grocer's before Hugh Keating had time to say goodbye properly. He looked at the roan mare, who had calmed down now she was no longer being harassed by an impatient rider. Hugh had been known to expend more energy on avoiding work than it would have taken to do the job in the first place. He patted Beatrix Verstappen's roan mare and led her away to the warmth of the livery barn.

'If Darrow had asked, I'd tell him to sort his own horse out,' Hugh confided to the horse. 'But Miss Beatrix is a pleasure to help out.'

The roan mare sighed companionably and walked quietly beside him.

On her way down Main Street, Beatrix Verstappen ran past the sheriff's office, but neither of the men inside noticed her. Sheriff Darrow was seated behind his desk, facing a sulky youth.

'For shame,' the sheriff drawled. 'Beating up on Billy Darwin like that.'

The bulky youngster, Sam Elliot, stared back defiantly. 'He's always bragging 'bout how the girls like him best.'

'So that makes it right for you to near on break his arm?' The sheriff's rich, Southern voice took on a menacing tone.

Young Elliot studied the edge of the desk but didn't reply.

Sheriff Darrow stood up. He wasn't unduly tall, but he carried himself well and was always neatly turned out. The only touch of colour in his grey-and-white clothing was the blue silk bandanna he wore as a cravat; even his Army Colt rode in a black leather holster. Right now, facing the hot-tempered delinquent, his dark eyes glittered dangerously, but Darrow could set ladies' hearts fluttering with a devastating smile when he chose. He stalked around the desk to Sam Elliot's side.

'Answer me, boy!'

'I didn't mean to do it!' Elliot retorted. 'Billy teased me; he kept on goin' on about it. I got fed up with it. I didn't mean no real harm.'

The flow of excuses came to a sudden end as the sheriff cuffed the youth smartly across the back of the head.

'You got a mighty mean temper, boy,' Darrow drawled. 'Just like your uncle. I done told you before about fighting and hurting folks.'

Elliot cringed before the sheriff's sharp tone. His uncle was the town's saddler; a powerfully built man who had been in trouble a few times because of his short temper.

Darrow gave the youth a contemptuous look. 'I could haul you up before Justice Robinson but I don't see why this one-horse town should waste its money on a fool like you,' he warned. 'This time I'm fining you five dollars. But if you start up any more fights, I will bring you up on charges of assault. Got that?'

'Yes, sir.' Sam Elliot could hardly get the answer out fast enough.

Darrow stepped back a pace. 'Give me the five dollars.'

Elliot got out his pocketbook and reluctantly parted with the money. Strictly speaking, the sheriff wasn't supposed to set fines himself, but Darrow claimed that a few dollars here and there discouraged petty criminals.

'Get out.'

Sam Elliot hurried out, not even stopping to put his hat on before going into the cold. Darrow tucked the five dollars into his jacket pocket. He got a share of all fines imposed by the justice but kept the money from his unofficial fines entirely to himself. The sheriff's pay wasn't bad by town standards but Beauchief Darrow had been born to the luxury and ease of a wealthy Southern family and he still vaguely resented the loss of all that during the Civil War.

The office door opened again and a young woman entered, closing it hastily behind her. Darrow's stern expression immediately softened as he came forward to help with the basket she was carrying.

'Good afternoon, Miss Davis.' He steered her towards the coal heater.

'Good afternoon, Sheriff,' Minnie Davis answered. 'Please excuse me for barging in like this.' She gazed around at the office as she spoke.

It was a pleasantly warm room, since both Darrow and Hugh Keating believed in keeping the heater well filled. There was a large, leather-topped desk, some well-made chairs, a safe, a sturdy filing cabinet, a rack of shotguns and rifles, and two home-made shelves which supported a row of law books, a tin mug and other odds and ends. A noticeboard by the door to the rear of the building held Wanted posters, a shopping-list and two cigarette-cards with pictures of showgirls in brief costumes, which Hugh had pinned up and which Darrow ignored.

'What can I do for you?' Darrow asked, setting the basket on the desk. 'I'm afraid Hugh isn't in at the moment,' he added.

Minnie's face fell slightly. 'I was intending to do something for you both,' she said. 'I thought your Christmas might be a little plain, with you two batching here, so I made you a dried-raspberry pie and a frosted cake.' As she spoke, she took the cover off the basket and lifted out the baked goods.

Darrow's face warmed. Minnie Davis wasn't pretty and her winter coat was a plain navy wool, probably home-made and not fashionable. However, her face lit up when she smiled and the sheriff admired her good nature and common sense.

'That's mighty kind of you,' he said. The gentle smile he showed her would have set hearts fluttering all over town, but Minnie did no more than to colour slightly.

'Hugh told me he liked white frosting best, so that's what I've done.' She paused, looking thoughtfully at the beautifully cooked, simple goods. 'They're not expensive or fancy I'm afraid . . .'

Darrow guessed what she was thinking. 'Why, I'm sure he'd rather have something you made than the fanciest baker's goods. If he wanted fancy desserts, he wouldn't be living out here in Govan still.'

'I guess not,' Minnie answered, cheering up.

Only Darrow had any real idea of what Hugh Keating's private income from his family was. There was no need for the Englishman to work, let alone live in a place as isolated and provincial

12

as Govan, but he stayed on in the town anyway.

Minnie lingered by the heater a moment, then moved away. 'I must get back; there's so much to do in our house yet. We've been baking all day.'

Darrow escorted her to the door. 'Thank you for your kind offerings. Give our best wishes to your family.'

She smiled a goodbye and was off, hurrying along into the cold wind. Sheriff Darrow picked up the cake and pie and took them upstairs, where he put them alongside the other festive treats baked for the bachelor lawmen by generous, considerate and hopeful women of the town.

★ ★ ★

In spite of what she had told Hugh Keating, Beatrix Verstappen hurried past the Wells, Fargo office and entered the railway depot building at the end of Main Street. Tim Judd was busy with the telegraph, tapping out a message

13

along the wires. He didn't even glance up as she quietly closed the office door. Smiling to herself, Beatrix tiptoed across the wooden floor until she was right behind Judd's chair. When he finished the message and leaned back, she covered his eyes with her gloved hands.

'Guess who?'

'Beatrix!' Tim Judd was on his feet in a moment, sweeping her into a hug.

Beatrix grinned up at him, aglow with pleasure. 'No one saw me coming in.'

'Let's go upstairs.' Judd led the way into his living-quarters.

If it was improper for an unescorted young lady to visit a man's private rooms, neither of them cared. Beatrix never cared about anything that spoilt her fun if she could get away with it, and Judd was too thrilled at having her attention all to himself.

Beatrix settled herself in the only armchair, letting Judd fuss over her, fetching a rug to keep her lap warm.

Tim Judd was good-looking in a bland way, with brown side-whiskers and light-blue eyes. He wore the plain, dull-coloured clothes of a man who doesn't know much about style.

'I'm late because my new horse was playing up,' Beatrix said. 'She's not outside. Deputy Hugh kindly took Paris to the livery barn for me.'

'It's too cold for a fine horse to be standing about,' Tim Judd agreed as he bustled about at the stove, fixing coffee for his enchanting guest.

'He was very sweet about it,' Beatrix said. 'He's a for-real English lord, isn't he?'

'Not Hugh.' Judd was one of Hugh's drinking and gambling cronies. 'His father is, but his older brother will inherit the title.' Judd felt it was time to change the subject. 'I'm happy you came,' he said with simple sincerity.

Beatrix sparkled at him instinctively, even while wondering how much the English deputy had in the bank. 'Meeting you is one of the best things about coming to live out here. I've never had such charming friends before.'

'You've certainly brightened the town up.' Judd poured coffee into his best china cup, added sugar, and handed it to his guest.

Beatrix held the cup under her nose and breathed in the warm smell. 'This is so good.'

Judd beamed with pleasure as he watched the lovely woman visiting his home. While they were drinking the coffee, Beatrix chattered on about the Dutch Christmas customs that her family had celebrated earlier in the month. She lived with her older brother, Henk, and their mother at the Bar M ranch. They weren't ranchers though; Henk had made his fortune with a string of jewellery shops which had expanded from the booming cowtowns into larger cities like Cheyenne and Denver. Judd listened politely but there was restlessness in his manner as he moved about the room.

'That sounds lovely,' he said at last. 'It'll be different next year though, won't it?'

'How do you mean?' Beatrix spoke lightly but without alarm.

Judd strode across to stand in front of her. 'Beatrix, I've said I want to marry you,' he reminded her.

2

Beatrix's pretty face lit up with a radiant smile. 'Of course I remember; I couldn't possibly forget that.'

Judd knelt down on the wooden boards so he was gazing up at her in a way that Beatrix found delightful. 'Well then,' he said.

'Well then what?'

'I want you to say yes. I want you to tell everyone that we're going to get married.'

'Oh, Tim.' She took his hand between her own. 'You're so kind and sweet.'

'That's not an answer.' His voice was firm but the anger melted from his soft eyes as he looked at her.

Beatrix started to take command of the situation. 'Let's not rush into things. There's a lot of other people to consider.' There was a look of gentle

18

concern on her face.

'You're twenty-one. You don't have to get your brother's consent,' Judd pointed out. 'I don't want to upset your family,' he added less impetuously. 'But I love you.'

Beatrix squeezed his hand, apparently overwhelmed by the emotion of the moment.

'Henk respects you,' she said. 'I'm sure I can talk them round.'

'Then say yes. Say it now,' Judd begged. As she hesitated, he spoke sharply. 'If you don't want to marry me then say so.'

'It's not that,' Beatrix insisted sweetly. 'But I can't say yes straight away. I don't want to spoil anyone's Christmas. You know Bill Jones and Tom Elliot are awfully fond of me too.'

Tim Judd did know; he was all too aware of it, especially Elliot, who was famously hot-tempered.

'Of course they are. And you're always so nice to them. But they'll have to know soon. It's unkind to let them go on loving you if you're going to marry me.'

'A little longer won't hurt.' Beatrix smiled brightly as she absently twirled a blonde ringlet around a finger. 'It is the season of goodwill.'

'What about goodwill towards me?' Judd demanded. 'I'm half sick with love for you, Beatrix, and you won't give me a straight answer.'

'That's unfair,' she answered with a flash of temper. The irritation was gone almost as fast as it had appeared, carefully concealed behind a charming smile. 'It's a terribly important decision for a young woman,' Beatrix said, studying her hands modestly. Judd instinctively backed off for a moment, aware that their behaviour was rather too passionate for good manners. Then frustration overwhelmed him again.

'I've given you long enough to make the decision, Beatrix,' he cried. 'If you don't want to marry me then just say so. Don't keep coming round here, calling on me and treating me like your fiancé if I'm not.'

'Oh, Tim!' she exclaimed, leaning forward in the chair to take his hand again. 'I don't want to hurt you.'

'You keep saying you don't want to hurt anybody, but you keep petting me, and Bill Jones, and Elliot. Now you've started talking about Hugh.'

'You make it sound as if I have a string of lovers,' Beatrix replied rather tartly, stung by a remark that was close to the truth.

Judd got to his feet. 'You do! And you won't choose any of us; you just encourage us all to keep worshipping you.'

Beatrix got to her feet too, flinging the rug aside. 'Tim Judd! That's a dreadful thing to say to a woman!'

'I bet you wouldn't marry any of them if they asked you,' Judd flung back. 'You want to keep as many men as possible hanging on your every word.' He was trembling with frustration and misery as he spoke.

A venomous look appeared on

Beatrix's pretty face. 'I'm leaving. And I shan't be coming back.' A threat to withdraw her favour always brought the men into line. It didn't work this time. Judd grabbed her arm as she moved past him.

'Beatrix! Marry me!'

She wrenched herself free. 'Why should I?'

'I'll tell the others how you behave,' Judd threatened, desperate not to have her walk away from him. 'I'll tell Bill, and Tom and Hugh and all the men in town. You don't want a good husband like a woman should; you just want a band of devoted worshippers to fetch and carry and to adore you. You take advantage of everyone.'

'You can't do that to me!' Beatrix exclaimed, her green eyes blazing with fury. 'You can't say those nasty things.'

'I damn well can,' Judd told her, hardly aware of what he was saying. 'You've played me for a fool long enough, but I'll see that people know all about you. I won't let you go on taking advantage of everyone.'

'You can't stop me!' Beatrix hissed. 'I'll get Henk to stop you.'

'Your brother hasn't got enough money to buy me off,' Judd retorted. 'This time you're not going to get your own way.'

Beatrix slapped him as hard as she could. While Judd was off-balance, she fled down the stairs. He didn't follow, but tears glittered in his eyes as he watched her go.

There were no tears on Beatrix's face. There was nothing but blind anger as she stormed back up Main Street in the gathering dusk, holding her long skirts up so she could move faster, and not caring a jot about who might get a glimpse of her ankles. How dare Tim Judd talk to her like that! Beatrix knew perfectly well how easily gossip would fly round a small town like this. She'd done it herself in other places. Even if Bill and Elliot didn't believe Judd, there were plenty who would like to hear nasty things about her. Beatrix's face drew into a scowl. She couldn't let some railway-depot man spoil her fun; she wouldn't! He was only a nobody; just one of the men who flocked round her. Well there had always been plenty of them, and there always would be. She always got her own way.

The outer doors of the livery barn were open, even on a cold day like this. Beatrix hurried through and halted, looking around for the owner or his stable boy.

'Hello! Is anyone there?' she called impatiently. Even as she spoke, she released her long skirts and automatically smoothed them back into place.

When Norman strode from his saddle-room to help her, she appeared calm enough, though there was still an edge to her voice.

'Saddle my mare, and do it quickly please,' Beatrix told the black barn owner.

'Certainly, Miss Beatrix.' Norman popped back into the saddle-room and came out with the heavy side-saddle in his arms. 'You might want to wait in there,' he suggested, indicating the saddle-room with his head. 'It's a sight warmer than anyplace else.

Beatrix nodded and went in to wait. She didn't stay by the coal heater, but stalked up and down the little room, swishing her whip against her elaborate skirts. The simmering anger was getting stronger the more she brooded on Judd's threats. Beatrix had seen in the past how quickly love could turn to hate. She wasn't going to win Judd's affection again unless she promised to marry him. Her lips drew into a narrow line at the thought. She didn't want to marry anybody at the moment, and it certainly wouldn't be someone as dull and poor as a railroad man when she did. She wouldn't let him spoil her pleasure! All her life, Beatrix had been adored and indulged. First her father, and now her older brother worshipped her and tried to make her happy. Beatrix had rarely been crossed by them or any other male, and she found

Tim Judd's threats unendurable.

Beatrix slapped her whip hard across the nearest saddle. The violent action took the edge off her anger for a moment, and she stopped to look at the heavy saddle, wondering whether she had damaged it. A quick glance reassured her, and from there her gaze wandered up to the bundle of bedroll and bags on the shelf above. The curved shape of a gunbutt sticking out of a kitbag caught her eye. Beatrix hesitated a moment, listening, then pulled the gun from the bundle. It was heavy and she needed both hands to lift it comfortably. One shot from it would keep Tim Judd silent for ever. Without thinking further, Beatrix slid the gun into one of the deep pockets of her skirt. It was uncomfortable but the elaborate folds of fabric hid it well.

A few moments later, Norman led the roan mare to the mounting-block just outside the saddle-room. Beatrix climbed up, settling herself comfortably around the curved pommels of the side-saddle.

'Take care, Miss Beatrix,' Norman said as he released the reins to her. 'I reckon the weather's turning colder.'

'I'll be going straight home,' Beatrix said. She gave him a dollar and rode out on to Main Street. Shouts and yells from the far end of Cross Street suggested that school was out for the day. Turning the roan mare north, Beatrix pushed her into a lope.

No one was about as Beatrix urged the reluctant mare through the cold water of the river that ran past Govan. Once on the far bank, she turned off the trail that led towards the Bar M and began circling the town. She took her time about it, staying out of sight as she crossed the railroad tracks and then the river again. The roan mare tried to refuse the second crossing, but Beatrix cursed her and struck her fiercely with the whip until the frightened horse plunged across the icy water.

'If you've made me miss him, I'll

have you shot!' Beatrix cursed.

The mare flattened her ears and cantered on, steaming in the chilly air.

Beatrix pulled her up behind the depot. Lamplight still shone from the office window. Beatrix slithered down from the saddle and tied the mare to a clump of scrub trees. Taking the heavy gun from her skirt pocket, Beatrix picked her way through the slushy snow until she was almost between the Wells, Fargo office and the depot building. From there she could see the depot door, while remaining out of sight from the street. With the gun in both hands, she settled herself to wait.

★   ★   ★

Hugh Keating was glad to be back in the warmth of the sheriff's office. He'd only come up from the Freight Car saloon, next door but one, but the weather was turning icy again as the light faded. He was still hanging up his hat and overcoat when Darrow spoke.

'Would you care to explain this?' There was plain menace in Darrow's voice as he placed an empty whiskey bottle on the office desk.

'It's a bottle,' Hugh answered promptly as he tried to remember where he'd left it. 'Popular in the distilling trade as a container for their products.'

'That's not what I meant!' Darrow yelled.

Hugh's explanations dried up rapidly.

'I found it under this desk this afternoon,' Darrow went on, his dark eyes fierce. 'I found it by kicking it over. In front of my visitor. Who was Justice Robinson.'

Hugh could picture the scene. Darrow and the local justice had never got on and it was a sure bet that Robinson would have made the most of the embarrassing situation. In spite of his own predicament, Hugh felt the urge to laugh. It must have shown in his face, because Darrow's disapproval turned to downright anger. The sheriff stalked around the desk, causing Hugh to back away hurriedly.

'Look. I'm really sorry about that.' Excuses and protests flowed from the Englishman. 'I tried to put it where no one would see it. I didn't know you were going to knock it over. And Robinson's a pompous fool; you've said so often enough yourself.' Hugh found himself backed against the wall and shut up.

The two men were much the same height but Darrow's graceful carriage and air of authority made him seem taller. The sheriff's darker hair and piercing eyes gave him a stronger presence than Hugh's unassertive manner and mild brown eyes.

Darrow halted just a foot in front of his quivering deputy. 'I don't like Robinson,' he drawled. 'And I for sure hate looking a fool in front of him.'

'Least said, soonest mended?' Hugh suggested.

From the deepening scowl on Darrow's face, it was clear that he still had plenty to say on the matter. Fortunately for Hugh, the conversation was terminated by a ragged series of gunshots from the end of Main Street.

3

Darrow moved first to the gun rack, and then to the coat pegs. 'Get a shotgun,' he ordered curtly.

Much as he hated danger and violence, Hugh was grateful for anything that took the sheriff's attention off him. He did as he was told, leaving the office with his coat still flapping open.

They could see figures gathered at the end of the street before they got there. Old Whiskers from the Wells, Fargo office was bending over a sprawled figure while the clerk from the merchant store held up a lantern. Whiskers straightened as the lawmen approached.

'Tim Judd,' he remarked. 'No need to call the doc.'

Darrow accepted the old-timer's assessment without argument and started to examine the scene. Tim Judd lay on his back, arms outflung just as he'd landed. Small patches of dark blood stained the fast-freezing snow. Two shots had hit him in the chest and others had struck the depot building behind him, leaving pale streaks in the weathered lumber.

Hugh gaped at the spread of shots. 'Whoever wanted to get Tim wasn't much of a shooter,' he remarked thoughtlessly. The gasp of disapproval from the store clerk alerted him to his error. 'I'm sorry,' he mumbled.

Darrow ignored the interlude. He took a lantern from one of the other onlookers gathering around and spoke to Whiskers.

'We'll go check for tracks. Hugh, you keep folks back and send someone for Josh Turnage.'

The sheriff moved off, letting the old-timer walk ahead. Whiskers was better at reading sign than anyone else in town, and the sheriff knew better than to get in his way. They walked away from Main Street until Whiskers stopped, bending to examine the marks in the slush.

'Someone waited here a little while,' he said, rising stiffly. 'I can't make out too much sign, the snow's too soft to hold shape, but the tracks don't look so big.'

They followed the indistinct marks over the railway line to the patch of scrub-trees.

'Hoss left here a while,' Whiskers said, searching as well as he could with only the soft lamplight. 'Got a black tail.'

He held up a long hair that had snagged on a branch.

'Half the horses in town have black tails,' Darrow remarked.

'You'rn too, iffen I remember right,' Whiskers chuckled.

The sheriff didn't answer, but watched silently as Whiskers finished his search.

'Not a big hoss,' Whiskers concluded. 'About fifteen hands, small hoofs, most likely well bred. Headed off to south of town.'

'But the killer could have turned off in any direction,' Darrow pointed out. His face was stern and unrevealing. 'We'll never find the trail in the dark. We'll just have to hope that there is something left in the morning.'

They returned to the others and found Josh Turnage, the new town undertaker, bending over the body. Darrow spoke quietly to him.

'Before you embalm the body, I want Doc Travis to take a look. I would like to know what size of bullet it was.'

'Of course.' Turnage was a lean man, often unnervingly intense and sometimes unnervingly outgoing. 'There's no hurry,' he said. 'They don't go off so fast in this weather.'

Darrow gave the undertaker a sharp look but it had no effect. He was pleased to see that at least Turnage treated the corpse with due respect as it was loaded on to a handcart for transport to the funeral parlour.

Hugh appeared at the sheriff's side. 'Poor Tim,' he remarked. 'Not much of a card-player but a thoroughly decent fellow. Who the heck would want to shoot him?'

'I don't know,' the sheriff answered. 'But I sure don't like having a killer loose in my town. I'll find whoever killed Judd and see they get what they deserve. I give my word on it.'

* * *

Tim Judd's funeral was held after Christmas on Saint Stephen's day. Fat white snowflakes drifted from the steely sky, spangling the dark coats and shawls of the townsfolk as they gathered in the burial ground beside the church. Parson Hermann spoke a good eulogy for the dead man, but wisely kept it short as the congregation stamped their feet against the cold. There were no family present to say goodbye; Sheriff Darrow had written a short letter to Judd's parents back in Indiana. As Josh

Turnage and his assistant, Joe, began to fill in the grave, the mourners drifted away.

Darrow found himself facing Justice Robinson. The town's lawyer and Justice of the Peace was a short man, with a face like a roughly made currant bun and dark hair oiled firmly into place.

'How is your investigation going?' he asked without preamble.

Irritation flared in Darrow's eyes, but his voice was even as he answered. 'There is little evidence; almost nothing that points towards anyone in particular.'

'What about the gun?'

Other mourners glanced at them but kept on going.

'The bullets that Doc Travis done recovered were .44 rimfires,' the sheriff said. 'So surely from a Smith & Wesson. Gilmour says he hasn't sold one in months. Folks mostly prefer the Colt.'

Hugh interrupted by tapping Darrow on the shoulder. 'I've got to go. The

Davises are expecting me for lunch.'

'Don't stay too long. You're doing the rounds this afternoon,' Darrow said.

'I know,' Hugh grumbled. 'But it will be a change to have some pleasant company for once.' He left before Darrow could answer.

Darrow didn't have time to think about Hugh's remark because Robinson spoke again.

'Have you discovered who might have wanted to kill Judd?' There was plain accusation of incompetence in his voice.

Darrow stood straight. 'I didn't really know Judd myself. And I felt that I surely couldn't drop in on folk and start interrogating them on Christmas Day.'

'Of course not,' Robinson answered stiffly.

The two men faced each other, mutual dislike clear in their stance and faces.

'Surely a murderer can't hide for long in a town as small as Govan,' Robinson said.

'The murderer rode a horse,' Darrow reminded him. 'He could be fifty miles away by now. But if he's in town, I'll surely find him,' he added.

Something in the sheriff's voice made Justice Robinson bite back the comment he had been about to make. Darrow's outspoken contempt for Govan was the main source of their antipathy, but Robinson suddenly saw that the sheriff took this murder as seriously as he did. Well, Darrow had pulled through for the town before.

'I'll take your word on that,' Robinson said.

★ ★ ★

It was still snowing by mid-afternoon, when Hugh Keating was doing the rounds of the town. The lawmen walked all round the small town, checking that things were as they should be. Lost children and belongings were returned and other minor problems were sorted. At night, they checked doors that should be locked and kept an eye on the saloons and the brothel. Hugh liked doing the rounds in good weather as it gave him the chance to meet and talk to all kinds of people. Today there was no one to be seen.

'All inside, by their fires,' Hugh grumbled to himself, tugging the collar of his thick overcoat up round his ears. 'Even the burglars and troublemakers have more sense than to be out in this weather.'

He was walking between the rows of small lumber-houses that had gone up to the east of Main Street. There was no sidewalk and he was picking his way through frozen snow made uneven by a myriad of hoofprints and wheel-ruts. Fresher snow drifted softly against any available surface. Hugh's foot slipped and he nearly went face first into the snow, only saving himself by some frantic arm-waving.

'This is stupid,' he said aloud. His breath clouded white around his face. Hugh had been round most of Govan and that was quite enough for one day. He turned towards Main Street where at least there were sidewalks where the going would be easier. It was only because he was paying so much attention to where he was walking that Hugh saw the little patch of ginger fur huddled against a stable wall. He stumbled across and picked up the bedraggled kitten. It lay limply in his gloved hands as he inspected it.

Hugh breathed gently into the kitten's face. Its eyes opened briefly and it gave a faint mew but that was all. The kitten's mother was possibly in the stable, but Hugh realized that it needed warming and drying off if it were to live. Clasping the kitten in both hands, he hurried back to the sheriff's office.

Light shone from the windows and a quick glance showed that Darrow was at the desk, reading one of his law books. Hugh hesitated for the first time, imagining the sheriff's reaction to the arrival of a kitten. Then he looked at the little creature, lying trustingly in his hands, and decided that saving its life was worth any trouble it might bring. All the same, he unbuttoned his overcoat far enough to pop the kitten in his jacket pocket, before entering the office.

Darrow barely glanced up. 'Surely you haven't been all round town in this weather?' he said sarcastically.

'Well I have,' Hugh answered, hanging his overcoat and hat on the pegs.

'Without your gun?' Darrow added, suddenly noticing that Hugh was unarmed.

'It hardly seemed tactful to wear the Webley to Tim's funeral,' Hugh retorted.

He could have collected it afterwards, as both men knew, but he didn't like wearing the heavy revolver if he didn't have to. Darrow let the point slide; he didn't expect trouble either. Hugh escaped from the office and hurried upstairs to their living-quarters.

This area was much cosier than the office and cells downstairs. There were shelves full of books, two bright rag rugs, a gilt-framed mirror and a pair of upholstered chairs comfortably arranged by a small table which held an expensive chess set.

Hugh went straight to the cook-stove and stoked it up by the poor light from the front window before lighting the oil lamp on the bigger table where they ate. The fire in the stove was normally kept banked up ready for quick use. The cast-iron stove was already warm to the touch when Hugh opened the oven door and popped the kitten inside. In a few minutes he'd got it towelled off and dry, ready for the milk warming in a pan. As he carefully held the soft, fragile creature in his hands, it began to purr. A smile of sheer delight spread across Hugh's face.

Downstairs, Darrow had no idea that their household had gained an extra member. He was studying one of the law books he had kept from his time at university just before the War Between the States had broken out. His reading was interrupted by a visitor.

The newcomer was a cowhand; a Texan, to judge from the star design carved into his fancy boots.

'Howdy there, Sheriff.' The Texan nodded amiably. He shook himself, sending little drifts of snow to the wooden floor.

'How can I help?' Darrow asked coolly.

'Someone done stole my gun,' the Texan complained. 'I left it with my thirty-years gatherings in the livery barn, but some cow-hocked, low-down thief done took it away.'

'What kind of gun was it?' Darrow asked, sitting straighter.

'A Smith & Wesson .44 rimfire,' the Texan told him. 'I ain't seen it since the day afore Christmas.'

4

The stable out back of the Bar M ranch house was surprisingly warm in spite of the snow banked up outside. Beatrix Verstappen lowered the woollen shawl she'd had round her head, settling it back on her shoulders. Her entrance brought the groom hurrying over, hastily brushing strands of hay from his hair.

'How is Paris?' Beatrix asked, making for the mare's box stall.

'Still very poorly, miss,' the groom, Nicholls, admitted.

The roan mare didn't come to the door of her stall as they approached; instead she stayed with her head low and her ears turned out sideways. She was heavily rugged up and the parts of her coat that were visible were harsh and damp. Beatrix didn't try to disturb her but asked anxiously after her horse.

Paris might be silly, but she was lovely to look at and Beatrix liked to have nice things.

'I reckon she got chilled in town, maybe in the livery stable there,' the groom said.

'That might be it,' Beatrix agreed. She knew full well that the mare had got chilled while they had been waiting for Tim Judd to leave the depot, but she wasn't going to take the blame herself. 'I guess her coat's too fine to cope with the winters out here.'

'Maybe so,' Nicholls agreed. He was simply relieved that he wasn't getting the worst of the blame from the mare's capricious owner.

Beatrix turned away from the stall. 'I couldn't ride her anyway in this wretched weather, so it doesn't matter too much.' She wrapped the thick shawl over her head again to leave. She was rather clumsy in her movement, favouring her right hand.

Her brother greeted her as she entered the hall of the ranch house.

'How's the mare?' Henk asked. He was much taller than his dainty sister, a ruddy-faced man with hair a few shades darker than Beatrix's dusky blonde colour.

'About the same,' Beatrix answered, stamping snow from her boots.

Henk took the shawl from her and hung it from the brass coat-pegs nearby.

'Would you like me to get a better groom for her?' he suggested.

'I doubt if they could do anything that Nicholls can't,' Beatrix replied as she swapped outdoor gloves for a delicate lacy pair. 'Besides, how long would it take to find and employ another one out here? And in this Godawful weather?' she added pettishly.

'Hush,' Henk said automatically. 'Mamma's just in the parlour. She wants you to pour tea,' he added more loudly.

Beatrix strode ahead of him into the parlour. It was one of the most elegantly furnished rooms for miles around. A few of the pieces were European, brought out from Holland when Whilhelmina Verstappen and her now deceased husband had emigrated almost forty years earlier. The rest was more modern, paid for by Henk as he built up the family business. Tea had been set on a small mahogany table between the chintz-covered easy chairs. Sweet cakes and buns were piled on dainty china plates as steam trickled from the silver teapot.

'Please pour ze tea,' Whilhelmina Verstappen told her daughter. Although she spoke English well, she had never lost the clipped edges of her Dutch accent. The resemblance between mother and daughter was clear, even though Whilhelmina's hair was now steel grey. There were lines on her soft skin, but it was easy to see that she had had all the charm and beauty that her daughter now possessed. Beatrix perched herself on one of the chairs and did as she was told. For once she was clumsy and got a warning to mind what she was doing.

'A lady is always graceful,' Whilhelmina Verstappen said. She herself was sitting bolt upright, a picture of ladylike demeanour.

'Yes, Mamma,' Beatrix murmured softly. It was only when raising the stolen gun to fire it two days before that she had realized that her hands were too small to get a proper grip. The recoil had badly strained her thumb and caused the bruising that she did her best to hide with gloves. Beatrix appeared calm enough to her mother and adoring brother as she poured the tea and stirred delicate cups, but anger was seething just below the surface. It was Judd's fault that her new horse was ill and that her hand hurt all the time. People might have believed his horrid accusations that she was leading men on, when she had only been friendly with them. As if she would want to marry someone like a railroad man or a saddle-maker! She forgot about Tim

Judd again as she remembered her meeting with the English deputy. He wasn't particularly handsome, though he did have nice brown eyes, she remembered. But he was rich, surely, and an aristocrat, and he would almost certainly spoil and adore her if she wanted him to.

'Henk,' Beatrix said aloud. 'I've had a wonderful idea. Let's have a New Year's party. We can invite people from the town.'

Whilhelmina Verstappen frowned. 'Ze notice is rather short, daughter.'

'Oh, please.' Beatrix aimed her appeal to her brother. 'We haven't had a social event here yet and we should return the invitations we've received.'

As always, Henk took her side. 'I think it's a good idea.'

'Very well. We shall discuss suitable people.' Mrs Verstappen had the last word.

★ ★ ★

There were only two places to buy a proper meal in Govan; one was Pinder's hotel and the other was Mrs Irvine's Eatery. Hugh leaned back as Mrs Irvine slapped a plate of Chinese fried rice on to the table in front of him; fragments of food bounced off the plate.

'There ye be going, Lord Nob,' she said crossly.

'I am not a lord,' Hugh snapped in reply. He had never got on with Mrs Irvine, who seemed to hold him personally responsible for all English land seizures in Ireland, no matter how often he told her that his family had never had any Irish estates, and he always disliked being called a lord. However, as his friends preferred eating at Mrs Irvine's, and the portions were generous, it was where he ate lunch.

'Is the weather going to stay like this?' Darrow asked Whiskers. He ignored the customary by-play between his deputy and the Irish woman.

At the question, Whiskers paused, a forkful of beans poised precariously above his plate. His pale eyes studied the snowy street and glimpse of sky above the buildings.

'Yep.' He rammed the mess of food into his mouth and chewed with pleasure.

'As informative as ever,' Hugh remarked, scooping up a spoonful of rice. They believed the old-timer without question. Darrow grimaced slightly; missing the warmer winters of his Southern past. Hugh looked out of the window and saw something more appealing than the frozen snow.

'There's Miss Beatrix and her brother,' he remarked, pointing with the spoon. 'She's not riding her new horse today.'

'Some fancy-bred roan, weren't it?' Whiskers asked.

'That's right; I took it to the livery barn for her when she came into town just before Christmas.' Hugh gazed through the window as Beatrix rode past on a bay horse. 'Did her package arrive all right?'

There was a moment's puzzled silence. 'A package for Miss Beatrix?'

'Yeah.' Hugh stared at Whiskers. 'She said she'd come into town to get something from your office.'

Whiskers shook his head. A fragment of egg flew off his greying moustache, making Darrow wince. 'Ain't been no package for Miss Beatrix, nor any of them Dutchies.'

Hugh leaned back in his chair, frowning. 'I'm sure that's what she said.'

'The only thing you're ever sure about is when your next drink is due,' Darrow remarked tartly. He nodded towards the window. 'You can ask her yourself. It looks as though she's coming in.'

A shot of cold air blasted into the warm eatery as Beatrix Verstappen entered, smiling at the three men as she crossed the room. All three stood up to greet her, Whiskers belatedly following the example of the other two. Beatrix was wearing a velvet-trimmed bottle-green coat that made her hair seem fairer, and a fashionable little hat decorated with ostrich feathers. Altogether, she looked like an illustration from the latest *Godey's Lady's Book*. Scrawny, middle-aged Mrs Irvine watched her resentfully from behind the counter.

'How nice to see you,' Beatrix said to the men, offering her hand to Hugh, who managed to be the nearest. He squeezed her tiny hand, and gave an exclamation of apology as she winced.

'It's not your fault,' Beatrix reassured him. 'It's rather bruised. I foolishly caught my hand in the chest of drawers,' she explained.

'I hope it gets better soon,' Hugh said, fetching a chair from the next table for her.

Mrs Irvine appeared, staring at Beatrix Verstappen with a particularly vinegarish expression.

'You want anything?' she asked abruptly.

Beatrix smiled prettily. 'Just some coffee please.'

Mrs Irvine grunted and went to fill the order.

'I'm glad to find you,' Beatrix said, smiling at Hugh, who grinned foolishly in return. 'We've had this marvellous idea. Mamma has said that I can have a New Year's party. We'd love you to come.' She looked at both Hugh and Darrow, but managed to avoid catching Whiskers' eye.

'I'd be delighted to,' Hugh answered with some enthusiasm. It hadn't escaped him that Beatrix was starting to pay more attention to the handsome sheriff.

'It would be nice to enjoy some civilized company,' Darrow answered, shooting a mocking glance at his deputy. 'Hugh's society sure leaves something to be desired.'

'I'm sure a born gentleman like Mr Keating must be good society,' Beatrix protested.

'There's a difference between a born

gentleman and being a gentleman born,' Darrow replied.

Hugh decided it was time to change the subject. 'Why aren't you riding your new horse today?' he asked. 'Is she still playing up?'

Beatrix shook her head. 'Paris has a chill, maybe pneumonia.' She was about to elaborate when Mrs Irvine appeared with an enamel mug full of strong black coffee, and carefully placed it on the table.

'This weather's mighty cold for a fancy-bred hoss like your'n,' Whiskers said.

'She took a chill when I was last in town,' Beatrix continued. 'I guess she got cold on the way home.'

'That was Christmas Eve, wasn't it?' Hugh asked suddenly. 'Have you heard the news about Tim Judd?'

Beatrix started, then took a deep breath. 'What news?' she asked anxiously.

Hugh hesitated, unsure of what to say. Darrow had noticed Beatrix's reaction, and watched her steadily as Hugh told her that Tim Judd had been murdered.

'Did he die right away?' Beatrix asked, clutching the coffee-mug.

'He did.' Darrow saw thoughts come and go in her green eyes. 'He took two shots full in the chest. He was surely dead before anyone could do anything for him.'

Beatrix studied the mug of coffee. 'That's awful,' she said quietly.

Hugh glared at Darrow; there had been no need to mention such details before a young lady like Beatrix. He patted her arm sympathetically.

Darrow ignored him and spoke to Beatrix. 'Were you acquainted with Tim Judd?'

Beatrix nodded. 'He was always kind to me.'

'He thought a great deal of you,' Hugh said. Darrow put his knife and fork neatly together on the plate and pushed it away. He stood up, fishing some coins from his pocket. 'I'm mighty sorry to have given you bad news,' he apologized. 'But I must be on my way.'

Beatrix looked up quickly. 'Will you attend our party?' Her eyes sparkled as she studied him.

Darrow suddenly smiled. 'Why, I believe I shall.' He stopped at the counter to pay Mrs Irvine, then left, fastening his grey overcoat.

Snow crunched under his boots as the sheriff walked up Main Street. He nodded politely to Hinchcliffe, who was standing in the window of his grocery store, but his thoughts were on the conversation in the eatery. Beatrix Verstappen had been in town on the day that Tim Judd had died, and she had lied to Hugh about the reason for her visit. It didn't take much to guess that a pretty, vain woman like Beatrix had been visiting a man, and wanted to keep it quiet. Darrow made his way to Norman's livery barn, wondering whether Beatrix Verstappen had seen anything that might help find Judd's killer.

The livery barn was warm and quiet inside. Darrow glanced into the saddle-room, but the owner was nowhere to be seen; he was probably at lunch. The sheriff passed time by visiting his sturdy black gelding. He had already checked the horses in the livery barn against the description that Whiskers had got from the tracks outside the railroad depot. The horses in Govan tended to be chosen for stamina and strength; none had the fine build that Whiskers had suggested. Darrow heard the outer door opening and went to meet the returning barn-owner.

'Good afternoon, Sheriff,' Norman greeted him cheerfully.

'Cold afternoon,' Darrow returned. 'If the snow gets worse. Gabriel should have less corn; I don't want him getting overheated.'

'Sure thing, Sheriff,' Norman answered, mildly annoyed at being told how to do his job. Darrow noticed the undertone of irritation but ignored it. 'I understand Miss Beatrix Verstappen left her new horse here on Christmas Eve?'

'That's so.' Norman made himself comfortable on the chair next to the stove. 'Fetched clean out from Kentucky on the railroads, poor Tim Judd said.'

'Expensive. What does this horse look like?'

'It's a lightweight roan mare, about fifteen one. Black mane and tail, black points and a white star plumb in the middle of her face. Miss Beatrix and that horse looked just as pretty as a picture,' Norman answered warmly.

The description matched the tracks near the depot better than any other horse Darrow had seen around Govan. What had Beatrix Verstappen been doing?

'I hear tell the mare caught a chill on the way back from town,' Darrow drawled. He sounded casual but, typically, he decided to act at once. 'I got work to do,' he remarked, turning to leave. The sheriff stopped in the door of the saddle-room. 'Oh, Hugh brought the roan mare in, didn't he? Who fetched her when Miss Beatrix left town?'

'Miss Beatrix came herself. Waited right in here while I saddled up for her.'

'What time?'

Norman thought. 'The kids had just come out of school, I remember.'

Darrow knew that would be about 3.30: Judd had been murdered an hour later.

'Did anyone else come in that afternoon?'

'I don't reckon so.'

'Thanks.' Darrow had just remembered that the gun which had killed Judd had been stolen from the livery barn's saddle-room that same afternoon.

5

Soft white flakes started falling from the grey sky as Beatrix hurried along the sidewalk. She glanced up, wondering whether to visit the parson's house and invite him to the party now, or whether she should meet Henk and go straight home. Her thoughts were interrupted by Sheriff Darrow, leaning out of his office door.

'Miss Verstappen? I'd like to speak with you for a moment.'

'Certainly.' Beatrix entered and stared around the sheriff's office with blatant curiosity. The sheriff indicated the chair in front of his desk, and moved around to his own seat. Beatrix turned her back and went to examine the Wanted dodgers on the notice-board.

Darrow was a gentleman and wouldn't sit down until she did; it was fun to keep him standing a little longer. The scraping of chair-legs on the wooden floor told her she'd guessed wrong. Beatrix gave up her little game and sat down herself, studying the sheriff. He was decidedly handsome and well-dressed, but there was something a little dangerous in his dark eyes and the calm way he watched her.

'What is it?' Beatrix asked, smiling prettily across the desk. The sheriff didn't smile, but Beatrix could see admiration in his eyes. Her confidence grew.

'I need to know what you were doing in town on Christmas Eve,' Darrow drawled. Beatrix started to answer, but the sheriff kept speaking. 'I know you lied about picking up a parcel. Where were you that afternoon?'

Beatrix felt a quick flush of anger; she wasn't used to being caught out and asked questions.

'I was in town on private business,' she answered primly.

Sheriff Darrow smiled. 'For shame,

trying to cover up your little adventures. What business could a for-real lady have that she can't tell others about?'

'I was . . . ' Beatrix suddenly remembered Tim Judd, and fell silent in confusion.

'Now would I be far wrong in assuming that a pretty lady like you might have been visiting her beau?' Darrow asked.

'That's none of your business!' Beatrix flung back.

'Of course not. But whoever you were visiting, you were near the railroad depot when Tim Judd was murdered. That roan mare of yours caught a chill while waiting around in the snow. There's not another horse in town would leave tracks like that.'

Beatrix had never considered that she might be found out. She fell back on her charm as she tried to pull herself together. She smiled prettily and wound a dusky blonde ringlet around her finger as she thought.

'Why, Sheriff. I guess you're right about why I was in town. I didn't want Mamma to know who I was visiting. She has some very old-fashioned ideas about who my sweethearts should be.' Beatrix gave him a conspiratorial look.

'I'll bet she does.'

Beatrix got the feeling the handsome sheriff was mocking her.

'Please don't let Mamma and Henk know I fibbed to them,' she pleaded. 'There'd be such trouble.'

Most men would promise anything when she asked them in that tone.

Sheriff Darrow merely made another demand. 'I don't care whom you see or don't see. I want to know whether you saw or heard anything of Tim Judd's murder.'

Beatrix was getting annoyed at Darrow's failure to fall for her charms and the mention of Judd's name did nothing to improve her temper.

'I was nowhere near the depot!'

'Your horse was.'

'That doesn't mean I was.'

'Well where were you then? Who were you seeing?'

'I wasn't seeing anyone!' Beatrix had had enough of this and stood up to leave.

'You have contradicted yourself again,' Darrow answered. 'That's surely a sign of a guilty conscience.'

'Oh!' Beatrix was temporarily lost for words. The last man to argue with her had been Tim Judd, and what a nuisance all that was turning out to be.

'Who are you sheltering?' Darrow asked. He rose too, walking around the desk. 'Is it the man who killed Judd? Did they fight over you perhaps?'

'I won't stand for any more of this!' Beatrix turned for the door. Her charm had failed and she had no other resources to fall back on.

Darrow swiftly moved to block her exit. 'Answer me or you won't leave.'

'You are no gentleman!' Beatrix exclaimed.

'So I've been told.' Darrow took Beatrix's arm. 'Who are you sheltering?'

'No one.' Beatrix was flustered; she couldn't think of any names or excuses. 'I'll tell Henk how you've treated me. He won't let you be so rude.'

'Tell me what you were doing in town after you left the livery barn.'

'I can't!' Beatrix shouted. She raised her hand to thump the sheriff in the chest, but Darrow calmly caught her slender wrist.

'Then I'm arresting you for obstructing the law,' he announced.

A moment later, the door crashed open. Henk strode in, Hugh trailing in his wake.

'What in hell's going on?' Henk demanded. He saw the sheriff holding his sister's arms and lunged forward, shouldering Darrow aside. 'You leave my sister alone.'

Darrow staggered back a pace. He was the same height as Henk but less heavily built.

'He was assaulting me,' Beatrix told Henk, her voice shaking.

'You dog!' Henk lashed out in a

swinging punch that caught Darrow right on the jaw. The sheriff was thrown backwards against his desk, scattering books. Henk rushed at him, grabbed his jacket and swung the lighter man around. Hugh stepped sideways fast as Darrow was thrown across the room.

'I say! I don't think you should be doing that,' he told Henk ineffectually.

Darrow finished up against the wall. He caught his balance quickly as Henk rushed in for another attack. Darrow dodged the first punch and rammed his fist heavily into Henk's stomach. The bigger man folded over, gasping as his face flushed darker. Darrow followed him, his eyes bright with anger.

'Don't you hurt him.' Beatrix rushed forward, swinging her riding whip.

Darrow glimpsed it as she aimed for his head, and twisted desperately aside. The whip cracked against his right shoulder, numbing it.

'Bitch!' he hissed. Henk recovered from his blow and advanced again. Darrow tried to deflect the punch but his arm was clumsy. Henk's fist glanced off his arm and the side of his face. Hugh danced around the group, reluctant to draw Henk's attention.

'Stop it.'

As Henk closed again, Darrow ducked. He pushed his shoulder into Henk's stomach and grabbed him round the legs. By lifting and shoving, he toppled the other man on to the floor. Henk landed heavily, momentarily winded. Darrow simply dropped, knees first, on to his belly. Henk retched at the brutal impact.

'You bastard!' Beatrix swung her whip.

With Henk out of the fight, Hugh finally got the courage to intervene. He impulsively grabbed Beatrix round the waist and lifted her up, swinging her away from the sheriff. She squealed with surprise and anger as he dumped her down again.

'I'm sorry,' Hugh apologized instinctively, then ducked as she swung the whip at him. Acting with remarkable speed, he grabbed the whip and twisted it from her hand. Beatrix gave a yell of pain and let go, nursing her bruised hand.

'Hugh!' Darrow was out of breath. 'Get the cuffs.'

Hugh did as he was told and advanced warily on Henk.

'Put them on her,' Darrow corrected, keeping an eye on the businessman.

Henk was still gasping unevenly, but his face was a more normal colour. He rolled on to his side, clutching his stomach as he watched Hugh reluctantly cuff Beatrix.

Darrow forestalled the inevitable questions. 'She surely knows something about Judd's murder, and she won't tell me who she's protecting. She stays under arrest until she talks.'

'I'm never telling you anything you want to hear,' Beatrix retorted defiantly.

Darrow shrugged, and told Hugh to put her in one of the larger cells. He stood up, working his stiff and bruised shoulder.

'Are you ready to talk sensibly?' he asked.

Henk glared at him, then nodded. He sat up slowly, wincing. 'I'll fix you good for this,' he warned.

Darrow returned his frosty look. 'We'll see.'

★ ★ ★

'I don't like it,' Hugh complained, pacing about the office, half an hour later.

'I'm not asking you to like it,' Darrow snapped. He was trying to write his report of Beatrix's arrest in the logbook, but his right arm was still stiff and clumsy from the whip blow. He dipped the pen into the ink-bottle and cursed under his breath as it blotted the page.

'Henk Verstappen's furious with us, and he's a big chap; he scares me.'

'I'd noticed,' Darrow said drily. 'You sure weren't rushing to help me.'

Hugh stopped pacing. 'If I'd tried to

help you he might have turned on me,' he pointed out. 'I'm not here to be a hero.'

'Or any use at all, so far as I can see.'

Hugh opened his mouth to argue, but heard footsteps stopping on the sidewalk outside. He glanced at the window and prudently moved further away from the door.

Henk Verstappen entered, accompanied by Justice Robinson. The businessman ignored the deputy, instead advancing on the desk where Darrow was working. Henk had tidied himself up after the fight, smoothing down his thick, light-brown hair.

'Sheriff Darrow, I want a full explanation of why you've arrested my sister.'

Justice Robinson stood alongside Henk Verstappen; the top of his head barely reached the other man's shoulder. There was no lack of courage in his black eyes as he faced the sheriff.

'This seems to be a most irregular act,' the justice said.

Darrow leaned back in his chair, inviting the others to sit.

'I'm looking into a murder case.' He looked at Robinson. 'I told you I'd get whoever killed Judd, and I for-sure intend to keep my word.'

'How does Miss Verstappen come into this?' Robinson asked flatly. Darrow repeated the evidence of the tracks, of Beatrix being the only one who could have stolen the gun, and of the horse having a chill from standing around in the cold.

'I know that she was near the depot when Judd was killed, but she won't tell me what she was doing, or who she saw.'

'Who my sister spends time with is her own business,' Henk insisted.

'If she's involved in a murder case, then it becomes my business,' Darrow answered.

Robinson nodded solemnly. 'We must have firm law and order in Govan.'

'He's arrested my sister!' Henk

exclaimed. 'Beatrix is a decent, modest lady.'

'Beatrix was almost certainly visiting her beau,' Darrow said.

Henk gave an exclamation of fury. 'My sister would never go visiting a gentleman unaccompanied! That might be the sort of thing your Southern girls do, but my sister is a lady.'

Darrow's eyes glittered but he held on to his temper.

'Who was she visiting then? Do you know what your sister was doing on Christmas Eve? She's lied once already.'

Henk turned to Justice Robinson. 'My sister is a lady, and it's not fitting for her to be held in jail here like a common thief.'

'Wait.' Robinson held up one plump hand. 'If Miss Beatrix was near the scene of the crime, and may have procured the weapon, I think the sheriff is within his rights to ask her about it.'

'He's got no right to hold Beatrix here.' Henk's face was flushing again.

'I can hold anyone I like for

obstruction of justice,' Darrow pointed out. 'I could arrest you too, on grounds of assault.'

Henk shot to his feet, causing Hugh to shrink further back into his quiet corner.

'Assault!' Henk exclaimed. 'You near on broke my ribs.'

'You attacked me first,' Darrow answered with maddening calm.

Henk glared, then whirled round. 'Deputy! You saw the sheriff attack me. You're a witness.'

'I . . . er.' Hugh glanced from Henk to Darrow like a frightened rabbit.

'You saw everything that happened,' Darrow said, his eyes glittering. 'You know that Henk and Miss Beatrix both assaulted me.'

'Well . . . ' Hugh's answer faded as Henk took a step towards him.

Justice Robinson intervened. 'This is enough!' He glared fiercely at all of them, his ugly face promising no patience with excuses. 'If you want your sister released, Mr Verstappen, I suggest that you tell her to answer the sheriff's questions. If she doesn't have anything to hide, then I don't see why it should be a problem.'

'It's an infringement of civil liberties,' Henk replied angrily.

'So's being shot,' Hugh put in. 'But Tim Judd can't complain to anyone.'

Darrow smiled wolfishly at his deputy's quick answer, which didn't improve Henk Verstappen's mood. The stocky businessman headed for the law-office door.

'After I've told Mamma about this, I'm going to Laramie to get the best lawyer in town; I'll go to Cheyenne if I have to. But I'm going to sue this no-horse town for wrongful arrest and you're going to wish you never spoke to my sister, Sheriff Darrow. I'll make you pay for every minute she spends behind bars.' He stormed out, slamming the door.

Robinson made to leave more quietly. 'I sure hope you know what you're doing,' he said warningly to Darrow.

76

'The Verstappens bring a lot of money into Govan.'

'What would you rather have?' Darrow asked. 'Money or murderers?'

Robinson left without saying good-bye.

Hugh sat down, his soft eyes anxious. 'We're going to be in awful trouble if Miss Beatrix doesn't know anything about Tim's murder. I don't see why she should be involved in anything like that.'

'That is because, in spite of your low tastes, you are a gentleman at heart,' Darrow said witheringly.

Hugh frowned, trying to figure out the insult. He gave up and rose, planning to visit his hidden kitten and feed it while the sheriff was busy.

'Like I said, I hope you're right. You'd better come up with some solid evidence, like that gun.'

Darrow fixed him with a glare. 'We had surely better find some evidence.' He put the emphasis firmly on the plural.

'As long as there's some evidence. Henk doesn't mean either of us well.' With that gloomy forecast, Hugh went upstairs.

Darrow returned to his report-writing. He had a nasty feeling that his deputy was right about Henk Verstappen.

6

That same night, Hugh woke from an uneasy dream. He lay huddled under the thick feather quilts, vaguely aware of a harsh, scouring sound filling the cold air. The ginger kitten snuggled against him and started to purr. Hugh realized that the noise outside was the sound of a blizzard, and fell asleep again, soothed by the purring.

The blizzard was still howling when he woke the next morning. All the nail-heads in the ceiling overhead were fuzzily white with frost. Hugh stayed where he was until he heard the sheriff stoking the coal-heater in the other room. Then he hurled himself out of bed, grabbed his clothes, and hurried through to get dressed next to the heater.

'I thought our old family house was cold in the winter!' he exclaimed, untidily tucking the woollen shirt into his trousers.

The fierce storm winds wailed and shrieked in the stovepipes. The windows were frozen white squares that let in just a little dim light.

'This may last a day or two,' Darrow said. He had not yet shaved, but otherwise looked immaculate. 'You'd best check on Miss Beatrix while I fix breakfast.'

'All right.' Hugh smoothed his hair before going down. He was back a few minutes later. 'It's perishing down there. We can't move the heater into her cell, because there's no place for the pipe. I think we should let Beatrix come up here for the day.'

Darrow cracked eggs into the frying-pan. 'I don't trust her; she's as stubborn as a bogged-down mule.'

Hugh gestured at the white window. 'Where's she going to run to in a blizzard!'

Darrow took the point. 'I guess you are right.'

Hugh paused. 'You do? Somehow that makes it all seem worthwhile,' he continued to himself as he picked up the bunch of cell-keys. 'Darrow actually admitted I was right about something. If only there'd been a witness.'

Darrow maintained a dignified silence.

The dim, blizzard-bound day dragged by slowly. Even with the heater and cook-stove both stoked, the wooden house was chilly. Hugh worried about keeping the kitten out of Darrow's sight, but it wisely spent most of its time sleeping under his quilts. When it did wake up to play, the howl of the storm outside covered the soft sounds of its paws. Hugh spent more of his time with Beatrix. He told her that she could read any of the books, but she barely glanced at the shelves, saying she didn't like novels. She preferred to talk, asking Hugh all kinds of questions about his family and home back in England. Hugh disliked speaking openly about his family's wealth, and lovely though Beatrix was, he didn't entirely miss the eagerness in her eyes as she asked about doing the season and other fashionable pursuits. Her delight in hearing about dances and silk gowns struck him as verging on the vulgar. Minnie Davis at least had better taste than to discuss money so eagerly.

After lunch, he managed to distract Beatrix by producing a pack of cards and performing his skilled magic tricks for her. Beatrix watched with delight as he made coins appear and disappear, picked chosen cards from the pack and juggled canned goods. She clapped and called for more.

'I have to warm my hands again,' Hugh said, holding them over the heater. Beatrix was in the rocking-chair, a rug that Minnie had knitted for Hugh over her lap. Darrow had been working at the table, but he shut the law books, stretched, and moved to the other easy chair. Beatrix ignored him, as she had all day. Hugh watched as the sheriff bent over the chessboard and moved one of the ebony pieces. Rubbing his hands together, Hugh joined him at the board and studied the new layout.

'You're after that knight, aren't you?' he remarked. He thought a moment longer, then moved one of his bishops.

Darrow calmly moved his rook and took a pawn.

'Oh,' Hugh said. He sat down, barely taking his eyes from the board. Darrow usually won, but Hugh won just often enough to keep it interesting for both of them.

Beatrix saw the men settle down, their attention on the game. Henk had tried to teach her chess, but she'd found it slow and boring. She got up and took a turn about the room, getting her circulation moving again, but Hugh didn't even glance at her.

Beatrix was bored, and wanted to go home. No doubt Henk was planning a way to get her out of here but he couldn't do anything until this wretched blizzard ceased. Beatrix had complete faith that her brother would solve her problems for her. The only thing she never needed help with was getting men's attention. She began practising the steps for the waltz turn, counting under her breath as she stepped, turned and stepped again. Her bootheels tapped on the lumber floor as she manoeuvred around the furniture. Within three minutes Hugh had forgotten his chess game and was staring at her. Beatrix pretended she hadn't noticed, and went on dancing until even Darrow had looked up. She stopped, smiling prettily as if embarrassed.

'I'm sorry, have I disturbed you?'

'Not at all,' Hugh answered instantly.

'I was just dancing,' Beatrix explained. 'I thought it might warm me up. I'm so cold inside.' She hugged herself, inwardly delighted at regaining his attention.

Hugh ran to make coffee, once more a slave to her charms. Darrow fixed her with a piercing look, and turned away.

Henk Verstappen and his mother were trapped in the remote ranch house together. The large heater kept the parlour sufficiently warm for them, while the maids and cook huddled round the range in the kitchen. Henk spent the first day pacing near the heater, unable to concentrate either on a book or on his business papers. His mother sat peacefully in her favourite armchair, a silk shawl around her shoulders and a warm rug on her lap. She was embroidering a cushion-cover with fine silks.

'Henk, do sit down,' she ordered, as her son paced about again.

'I'm only trying to get my circulation going,' Henk complained, sitting down.

Mrs Verstappen threaded her needle. 'I hope zey are keepink Beatrix warm enough.'

'They'd better,' Henk growled. 'She's delicate.'

Beatrix had barely been ill a day in

her life, but Mrs Verstappen didn't correct him.

'I only hope zis will not spoil her reputation. If she loses her good name, we will not be able to get her married.' She started outlining a silk rose on the cushion.

'I don't think Beatrix wants to get married just yet,' Henk dismissed the idea.

His mother stitched steadily. 'She iz twenty-one. I was married to your dear pappa at seventeen. If Beatrix does not marry, people will be callink her an old maid.'

Henk scowled, hating the thought of sharing his sister. 'There's no one round here good enough for her.' It was what he had said about the last town they had lived in.

'She should get married,' Mrs Verstappen repeated. 'After all, I will haf you to take care of me, Henk.'

'Of course.' Henk leaned over to kiss his mother's soft cheek. 'Always, Mamma.'

'Goot.' Mrs Verstappen smiled fondly at her sturdy, handsome son.

The show of affection raised Henk's spirits. He stood up again to stoke the heater.

'Just as soon as this blizzard eases up, Mamma, I'll go to Laramie.'

'Maybe we do not need to spend ze money on a lawyer,' Mrs Verstappen said.

'I'll spend anything to help Beatrix,' Henk promised recklessly.

His mother frowned. 'I know. But you say to me zat ze sheriff is holdink Beatrix because he does not know where she was when zat man was being murdered. You should go to town and arrange somezing for her.'

'Fake an alibi?'

His mother shrugged. 'Talk to Beatrix first. She can tell you which men will lie for her. Zere will be one at least.' She calmly worked the petal of a silk flower.

Henk's face darkened. 'Mamma! You sound like that God-damned sheriff.

He was accusing Beatrix of having a string of beaux.'

Mrs Verstappen quelled her son's ill temper with one glance. 'I zink zat ze sheriff was right. Now use one of zese men to make an excuse for her.'

Henk was silent for a few minutes, seething with jealousy.

'If Beatrix stays in ze jail while we wait for lawyers, ze people in town will think her no goot, and zey will not receive her,' Mrs Verstappen said shrewdly. 'Get Beatrix out first, and zen call a lawyer to sue ze sheriff.'

Henk sighed. 'All right.' His concern for his sister's reputation won out, as his mother had known it would.

Whilhelmina Verstappen cut the silk thread and smoothed the cushion cover over her lap. Like Beatrix, she was used to having her own way.

* * *

'Doesn't it seem quiet?' Hugh remarked, entering the office for the first time in three days. The howling winds and the noise of frozen snow pounding the lumber building had gone, along with the frigid chill of the blizzard.

'The blizzard was not that noisy,' Darrow drawled. 'Not to someone who has to live with the sound of your voice day in, day out.'

'If I was annoying you, you should have gone out for a walk,' Hugh retorted.

'I considered it. Now go do the rounds.'

Hugh sighed as he picked up his coat and hat. Outside, the sun glittered brilliantly on the mounds of frozen snow that had banked up high against buildings and sidewalks. The town looked half-smothered by the encroaching whiteness. Hugh tugged the brim of his hat over his eyes, and almost collided with Henk Verstappen, who was hurrying in to see his sister. Henk didn't even bother stopping to greet the deputy. Hugh decided to let Darrow deal with Henk on his own, and began picking his way along.

He hadn't gone far when he spotted a familiar figure outside Van der Leo's store opposite. Hugh trotted over the street, the firm snow creaking under his boots.

'Minnie!' he called. 'How are you . . . all your family, I mean?'

Minnie Davis smiled at the Englishman as he clambered on to the sidewalk. Her blue winter hood hid the braided coils of mousey hair but her eyes sparkled with pleasure as she greeted Hugh. They talked about the blizzard, of course, just like the other groups of friends and neighbours who had stopped to talk in the street.

'Is it true Beatrix Verstappen is at the jailhouse?' Minnie asked eventually. When Hugh nodded, Minnie said. 'She always looks pretty, doesn't she?'

'Oh yes,' Hugh answered with naïve enthusiasm. 'Beatrix always looks lovely and she knows how to be perfectly charming.'

'I expect she does.'

Hugh failed to notice Minnie's mild sarcasm. 'Beatrix is fun to be with.'

'It's just as well, if she's under arrest. You'll be seeing a lot of her.'

'Yes. Well . . . I don't know.' Hugh was suddenly aware of having lost Minnie's approval. The situation promptly went from bad to worse.

'Hugh! How nice to see you, pet,' called another voice.

Hugh stifled a groan as Queenie joined them on the sidewalk. She was a plump, rather brightly-dressed woman who worked at Amy Vialla's place, the local whorehouse. Queenie was from the north of England and although Hugh always denied that he was a lord, she knew an upper-class voice when she heard one.

'How are you keeping?' she asked, squeezing his arm. 'You don't come around like you used to do. He couldn't keep away from me,' Queenie confided to Minnie.

Hugh detached himself, blushing.

'I've been terribly busy with work,' he said feebly.

Queenie hadn't missed the jealousy in the other woman's eyes. 'Did you like the biscuits I baked you for Christmas?' she asked Hugh. Queenie was determined to marry herself into some money.

'I had lots of nice things,' Hugh prevaricated.

Minnie picked up her basket. 'Do excuse me, I must be getting on with the shopping. We need yeast and more sugar and there's none in this store.'

Hugh was surprised. 'Van der Leo's a good merchant. I've never known him run out.'

'People bought a lot for the Christmas celebrations. He's expecting a delivery by train, but they've been held up. There hasn't been one through today.' Hugh glanced at the silent station at the end of Main Street. 'I'll go speak to Judd, I mean Appleton,' he corrected himself. His face fell as he remembered Judd's death. Minnie saw the sorrow in his expressive brown eyes and her heart warmed. She determined not to let herself be pushed away from Hugh by anyone else, at least not without making a fight of it.

'Take care,' she said, patting Hugh's arm affectionately. 'And thank you so much for my Christmas present, Hugh,' she added for Queenie's benefit. 'It looks just lovely on my dressing table.'

'Thank you.' Hugh smiled as she left. 'I'm doing the rounds now, so I can't stop to talk,' he told Queenie with unusual firmness. Tipping his hat politely to the prostitute, he walked away from her.

He found the new depot-manager energetically shovelling snow from the low platform beside the tracks. Victor Appleton was a sturdy, tall man, with a crop of unruly, dark blond hair. As Hugh hailed him, he turned and wiped sweat from his face with the end of his red muffler.

'Good to get out again,' Appleton exclaimed, leaning on his shovel. 'Get some good, fresh air into your lungs.'

'Marvellous,' Hugh agreed with less enthusiasm. He introduced himself and they shook hands. 'I've been told that the trains aren't running yet,' Hugh said.

Appleton nodded. 'That's so. Deep cutting between here and Laramie's all filled with snow. Take a day or two to dig it clear. All frozen, y'see.'

'Don't they have snowploughs?'

'Got to bring them out from further east. Might round up some men and make a start from this end.' He looked at Hugh speculatively. Appleton was good at sweeping others along with his brisk energy, but Hugh Keating could be just as quick off the mark when it came to excuses.

'I've got to finish making the rounds,' he said, turning to leave as he spoke. 'Good luck.'

Appleton didn't wait to see him go, but returned to snow-shovelling at once.

7

Back in the sheriff's office, Darrow had let Henk through to see Beatrix at once, but soon found himself confronted with another visitor.

'You can go in when her brother leaves,' he told Bill Jones. The sallow-faced schoolteacher meandered restlessly around the office. He took off his hat and smoothed down his hair, which already shone with some kind of oil. The attention to appearance didn't escape Darrow's notice, but the sheriff kept his thoughts to himself. As soon as Henk reappeared from the back, Bill Jones hurried past him to the cells. The two men exchanged a brief nod, making eye contact for a moment, but nothing was said. Darrow rose at a more leisurely pace.

'I trust you are satisfied with your sister's health?' he enquired.

'I shall be off to Laramie when I can,' Henk repeated. He stood beside the sheriff a moment, twisting a signet ring on his little finger. 'I think Beatrix will be home where she belongs soon.'

Darrow inclined his head. 'I must go and speak with Jones for a moment.'

They separated, Henk leaving the office. Darrow strolled through to the cells in the back of the building. Bill Jones was leaning up against the steel bars that fronted the cell, his attention wholly on Beatrix, who was sitting demurely on the end of the bed.

'I'm not used to receiving company when I look so untidy,' she was saying. It was true that her dusty blonde hair was loosely pinned, rather than elaborately styled as usual, but she looked like a beauty playing the part of being unkempt.

Jones produced a package from his pocket. 'I brought some of your favourite candy.'

'Oh!' Beatrix bounced to her dainty feet. 'Bill, I've so missed the taste of anything sweet.' She smiled enchantingly at him as she took the paper bag. 'You're far nicer than I deserve.'

Darrow's mouth twitched at her exclamation. During the blizzard, Beatrix had shown an insatiable appetite for pancakes with maple syrup. She had announced that she had no idea how to cook, as she had servants to do that, and had been content to tell Hugh what she liked best and wait while he served her.

Beatrix saw him and recognized the humour gleaming in his dark eyes. 'You can go away, Sheriff Darrow,' she snapped, her eyes flashing.

'And leave you two unchaperoned?' Darrow drawled insolently. 'Why, that wouldn't be at all proper. I must think of your reputation, Miss Verstappen.'

Beatrix looked as though she were about to stamp her foot in frustration.

It was Bill Jones who turned to the sheriff. 'Miss Beatrix is locked on the other side of these bars,' he said, his voice betraying his anger. 'I think she will be quite safe.'

'I reckon she is,' Darrow answered. 'But those bars won't protect you from all that sweetness.' With that, he left them alone to talk.

Bill Jones stayed in the back for ten minutes. Darrow was thinking of intervening when the door opened and the schoolteacher came back through. Jones took a few paces towards the desk, then turned away. He paused, then affected an interest in the notice-board on the back wall. Darrow said nothing, but let him fret. Jones lifted a notice to see an older one underneath, inspected Hugh's show-girl cigarette-cards with more attention, then abruptly turned away. He rocked back and forth on his toes, then strode purposefully towards the heavy desk.

'Beatrix was with me,' he blurted out.

Darrow looked up curiously. Jones's sallow face was faintly flushed.

'When?'

'Christmas Eve, of course.' Jones

evidently expected some exclamation from the sheriff, but Darrow's self-possession didn't waver. 'After leaving the livery barn, Bea . . . Miss Beatrix, visited me.'

Darrow showed no sign of noticing the hasty correction to the formal use of her name.

'You live on Cross Street,' he remarked to the teacher. 'Why, that's the opposite end of town to where she tethered her horse. Why take her horse from the livery barn to the depot, and then walk back so far?'

From the expression on his face, Bill Jones had no idea either.

★   ★   ★

Hugh Keating headed back along Main Street at a brisker pace than usual. It occurred to him that if the trains were going to be delayed, it would be as well to visit the stores before stock ran too low. Some dried fish for the kitten would be a good idea. He was trying to remember what was left in the store-cupboards, and making a mental note to buy more maple syrup, when he heard someone calling his name. It was Elliot, who ran the saddler's store almost opposite the law office. Elliot was leaning through his door, beckoning.

'I needs to speak to you, Deputy,' he said.

'What is it?' Hugh said warily. People who called him 'Deputy' were usually about to ask him to do something difficult. Elliot beckoned him inside the store, which smelt pleasantly of leather and saddle-soap.

'I got something to say.'

Hugh closed the door behind himself and waited. Elliot was a powerfully built, handsome man with black hair and a broad nose. He put Hugh in mind of a prize bull that his family had owned. Much as he loved gambling, Hugh always thought twice before playing cards with Elliot, who was a notoriously poor loser.

Right now, Elliot was glowering at

the deputy. 'Sheriff Darrow don't have no right to do what he did,' he muttered accusingly.

'Of course not,' Hugh answered instantly. 'What's he done?'

'Arresting Miss Beatrix, of course!' Elliot advanced on Hugh, who retreated towards the windows. 'If I'd been there when he done it, I'd have torn his head off!'

'I'm sure,' Hugh muttered, uncomfortably aware of just how powerful Elliot was.

'It ain't right, picking on Miss Beatrix like that,' Elliot rumbled. 'A for-real lady like her wouldn't do no wrong.'

'I'm sure she wouldn't,' Hugh agreed vigorously. 'It's all a mix-up, old chap.'

Elliot stopped, and nodded. 'She weren't at the depot. She was with me.'

'With you?' Hugh felt a mild stab of jealousy.

'Miss Beatrix came to visit and wish me well for Christmas. That's all that happened,' Elliot insisted, his deep voice turning threatening again.

'I'm sure,' Hugh assured him hastily. His face brightened. 'We can go and tell Darrow right now. He's only holding Beatrix until he finds out what she was doing.' Elliot nodded and picked up his hat.

The two men crossed Main Street together, Hugh slipping on the frozen snow as he jogged to keep up with the taller man. He flung open the office door.

'Hello, Bill,' he said to the schoolteacher, who was standing in front of the desk. 'I've got some good news,' he added proudly to the sheriff. 'I've solved your mystery for you.'

'Have you now?' Darrow drawled, glancing at the man who'd followed Hugh.

Elliot strode over to the desk, giving Bill Jones a nasty look. 'You're no gentleman,' he told the sheriff.

Darrow returned his stare evenly. 'I sure don't recall boasting about it to you.'

'You've put yourself clear in the wrong, arresting Miss Beatrix.'

Darrow stood up. 'You're the third man today to tell me that. Or rather, the fourth. I was forgetting Hugh, but then that's easy enough.'

'It is when you've got your nose stuck so high in the air you can't see anything below your hat-brim.' Hugh gave as good as he got for once.

Elliot ignored the habitual sniping between sheriff and deputy. 'I've half a mind to shoot you down, for arresting Miss Beatrix,' he told the sheriff fiercely.

Darrow was unimpressed. 'I'm sure that's all you have,' he answered.

'Goddamn you!' Elliot paused, calming himself. 'You can damn well let her out now because she was with me Christmas Eve, and nowhere near the depot.'

A cold smile showed on Darrow's face as he glanced from the saddler to the schoolteacher. 'Well now,' he drawled. 'It seems Miss Beatrix was plumb busy on Christmas Eve. It seems she was visiting with both of you at once.'

The two men stared at one another.

'You fool!' Elliot exclaimed, raising his fist.

'I got here first,' Jones retorted, his sallow face flushed. 'Henk came and arranged . . . ' He shut up suddenly and stared at his boots.

'Henk arranged for you to be an alibi for his sister,' Darrow drawled with satisfaction. He turned to Elliot. 'And you came in with the same idea, not knowing they'd already set something up. I surely hate to disappoint your gallantry, but I don't happen to believe either of you.'

'I'm telling the truth!' Elliot slammed his fist on to the desk, making the heavy inkstand jump. 'You got to let Miss Beatrix out!'

Darrow glared at him. 'I'm the law around here and I don't have to do anything I don't wish to.'

'You might be the law, but you're a

yellow curdog,' Elliot rumbled, shaking his fist.

Bill Jones tried to intervene. 'Elliot! There's no cause to lose your temper. Henk Verstappen's gone to get a lawyer.'

The powerful saddler turned on him. 'You stay out of this, you runt. It ain't none of your business what happens to Miss Beatrix anyhow.'

'I surely hate to see a grown man making a fool of himself over a woman,' Darrow drawled.

Both men turned on him but Elliot overrode the schoolteacher's protests. 'Miss Beatrix is a fine lady and you ain't fit to talk about her.'

A dangerous gleam came into the sheriff's eyes. 'I could arrest you for insulting an officer of the law,' he warned.

Elliot stormed away from him, roaming the room. Hugh pressed himself against the door, hoping not to be noticed.

'This ain't right,' rumbled Elliot, his

face as black as thunder. 'This surely ain't right.' He halted, half-turning to see the sheriff. 'Are you going to release her?'

'No. Beatrix Verstappen has refused to tell me what she was doing at the time of the murder, why her horse was tethered near the victim's house, and why she lied about her activities. She's trying to protect someone and both of you misguided fools are trying to protect her. All three of you deserve each other,' Darrow added witheringly.

Elliot was standing near the coat-pegs on the outer wall of the sheriff's office. Darrow's overcoat and hat hung there, along with his gunbelt. Elliot lunged forward and snatched the Colt from its holster. Hugh barely had time to realize what was happening, and to start reaching for the gun under his coat, when Elliot grabbed his shoulder and pressed the Colt against the deputy's head. Hugh froze instantly, his eyes round with fear. Darrow and Jones also stopped their moves. The schoolteacher was obviously alarmed; the sheriff was furious.

Elliot hauled Hugh into the middle of the silent room, his stolen gun resting firmly against his prisoner's head. 'Get the cell-keys,' he snarled.

Darrow's voice was carefully controlled. 'Let Hugh go. You're getting yourself deeper and deeper into trouble, Elliot.'

'Get the cell-keys!' Elliot pressed the gun harder against Hugh's temple. Hugh gave an involuntary whimper but made no effort to struggle against the taller, stronger man. Darrow opened the desk-drawer and removed a bunch of long keys.

'Jones, you get Hugh's gun and toss it into the corner. Do it slowly,' Elliot warned. Jones did as he was told, not daring to try turning the heavy Webley on Elliot.

'Now through the back. Let Miss Beatrix out.'

Darrow did as Elliot told him, though his face betrayed his silent fury.

Bill Jones followed at Elliot's curt signal.

Beatrix stood up as they entered the rear of the jailhouse.

'What do you want, Sheriff?' Her expression changed as she saw the other men. Jones moved aside and let her see Elliot's gun pressed against Hugh's head. 'Tom,' she said to Elliot. 'What are you doing?'

'What no other man in this town's got the guts to do. I'm getting you out of here.' Elliot jerked his head to the cell door. 'Let her out.'

Darrow advanced to the cell, the keys in hand. He looked straight at Beatrix.

'This won't work,' he said. 'Do you want to spend your life on the run?'

The excitement left Beatrix's pretty face, dying completely as she took in the look of abject fear on Hugh's face.

'Tom, I'm not sure . . . ' she started.

'Just do like I say,' Elliot snarled, giving Hugh a shake. 'We'll get married an' then you can't testify against me. I'll take all the blame for everything and you'll be safe.'

'Married?' Beatrix exclaimed. Darrow recognized the stubborn look in her green eyes.

'Just do as Elliot says,' he ordered sharply, putting the key in the lock.

Beatrix disliked Darrow, but she wasn't stupid.

'All right.'

She gathered up her coat and bonnet as the sheriff unlocked the cell. As soon as it was opened, she stepped towards Elliot but Darrow grabbed her arm, shooting her a warning look. Beatrix dropped her idea of getting close enough to distract the saddler, but kept talking.

'Oh, Tom. I can't believe you'd do anything so brave as this. And for me!'

Elliot spared her a brief glance before ordering Darrow and Jones into the cell.

'When I tells you, you lock the door,' he told her. He shoved Hugh so hard the deputy stumbled into the cell and almost collided with Jones. Elliot's gun pointed unwaveringly at Darrow.

Beatrix closed the cell door and locked it slowly.

'Good. Now come on.' Elliot took her arm and led Beatrix into the office.

'God's teeth I'd like to whip that stupid, besotted, bull-headed . . . ' As the front door of the jailhouse closed, Darrow let fly a string of curses aimed at Elliot.

'I quite agree,' Hugh said. 'But you still bungled that.' His face was pale, but he seemed to have recovered his spirits.

'You were wearing a gun but you didn't manage to stop him,' Darrow retorted.

'I like my head the shape it is.'

Jones intervened. 'We'd better yell for help; someone might hear us.'

'There's no need.' Hugh got up and rummaged under the thin mattress. He produced a short piece of wire, and went to tackle the lock.

8

Darrow watched with a disbelieving expression, but Hugh's unusual air of confidence kept him quiet. Hugh worked steadily for a minute until the padlock clicked open.

'Where did you learn to do that!' Jones exclaimed.

'Boarding school.' Hugh neatly hid the length of wire away. 'I thought this might happen sooner or later.'

Darrow didn't hang around to praise his deputy, but went straight to the rifle rack and started loading shells into his Winchester. 'Stop congratulating yourself and move.'

Hugh joined him, picking up his Webley and then a shotgun. 'What's your plan, O fearless leader?'

Darrow ignored the sarcasm. 'We'll tackle him from different directions. You keep him talking while I use cover to get the drop on him.'

Hugh looked serious. 'You want me to walk out there and strike up a conversation with a lunatic carrying a gun? He already threatened to kill me, if you hadn't noticed.'

'He only threatened you.' Darrow hauled on his overcoat. 'Elliot isn't a gunman.'

'Neither am I. And he's got a nasty temper, too.'

'Then your conversation had better be fascinating.' Darrow peered through the window before opening the door for his deputy.

Hugh stepped outside reluctantly and dithered on the snowy sidewalk, peering up and down the quiet street, until he thought to check for footprints. Clear marks showed that the fugitives were heading to the livery barn. Hugh remembered Elliot's threat to make Beatrix marry him, and started walking more briskly.

Inside the law office, Bill Jones picked up a shotgun and followed the sheriff to the back door.

'You're asking Hugh to take a big risk, facing Elliot,' he said.

'He just has to keep him talking while I get the drop on Elliot from behind,' Darrow snapped, letting himself out.

Jones closed the door behind them. 'You know what a vicious temper Elliot's got.'

Darrow answered quietly but forcefully. 'The Elliots all shout and break things, but they're not killers.' He paused by the alleyway between the law building and the grocer's. Hugh appeared at the other end, walking past along Main Street. Darrow slipped behind the grocer's, the snow crunching under his boots, and jogged over Cross Street. The livery barn was at the north end of town. Darrow walked parallel to Hugh's path, but behind the buildings that lined Main Street. He reached the rear door of the livery barn without trouble, Bill Jones a few paces behind.

The sheriff listened for a moment

before cautiously opening the door. He eased through the narrowest gap possible, the rifle held ready for use. The livery barn was warm after the freezing air outside, and smelt of straw and horses. It was also dim after the glitter of sun on snow. Darrow pressed himself against the nearest stall-door and peered along the central aisle, waiting for his eyes to adjust. He could make out three figures at the far end, standing near the office and the feedroom. Beatrix's full skirts made her easy to pick out; Darrow paid her no attention. Elliot had his back to the sheriff and was talking to Hugh. Darrow couldn't hear what his deputy was saying, but Elliot's angry answers were clear enough. He began to stalk closer, one careful step at a time.

Elliot's voice rang out in the quiet stable. 'Iffen you don't walk away now, I'll give you a taste of lead, goddamn it!' The saddler was pointing his Colt at the deputy. Hugh had his shotgun at waist height, aimed roughly in Elliot's direction. He spoke quietly, doing his best not to provoke the angry man further.

'You can't just steal Beatrix away with you and make her marry you. It isn't fair on her, is it?'

Darrow was concentrating so hard on the men he was approaching, that he didn't notice he was passing his horse's stall. The black saw him, and let out a friendly whicker of welcome. Darrow froze, his finger tightening on the trigger. Elliot was too busy with Hugh to pay any attention to the horses behind him.

'Miss Beatrix loves me,' Elliot insisted.

Beatrix looked as if she wanted to contradict him. Darrow hoped frantically that she'd have sense enough not to upset Elliot further. She must have believed Elliot's threats because she kept quiet, switching her gaze anxiously between the two men. The sheriff started creeping forward again. He knew he could hit Elliot from halfway down the barn, but he understood the impact of being threatened from just a few feet away. He wanted, if possible, to be almost within arm's reach of Elliot before he made his presence known.

Hugh was still talking to Elliot. 'All the same, a woman like Miss Beatrix looks forward to her wedding, and having her family around her. You don't want to spoil all her dreams,' he went on. His face was pale, but his stubbornness kept him doing his duty in spite of his fear.

Elliot didn't answer straight away, and for a moment Darrow thought Hugh's common sense had won through. Then Elliot let out a yell of rage and frustration.

'That ain't the point! You an' that miserable sheriff were holding Miss Beatrix in jail and that's just plain wrong. I'm the only one in this town with the guts to do anything about it. You aim to stop me, you yellow English lord?'

Darrow knew how Hugh would

react. He stopped where he was and snapped the rifle to his shoulder.

'Now look,' Hugh snapped, moving his gun slightly. 'I'm not a lor . . . '

Elliot just saw the movement and fired. Darrow saw Hugh buckle under the impact and fall limply, before the sheriff got his own shot off. It hit Elliot high in the back, staggering the big man. Darrow vaguely heard Beatrix screaming as he kept his eyes on Elliot. A smaller man would have fallen, but the saddler kept turning.

'Drop it!' Darrow ordered, working the rifle's lever action.

Elliot roared in blind fury, bringing his stolen gun round. Darrow wasn't inclined to take chances. He fired again, this time taking Elliot in the head. The saddler twisted and fell backwards, dropping the sheriff's Colt.

Beatrix was pressed against the wall of the saddle-room, shaking as she stared at the sheriff.

'Don't shoot me!' she wailed, her composure gone.

'Don't be stupid,' Darrow snapped. He advanced on Elliot, his rifle at the ready, but his second shot had blown the side of the saddler's head off.

'Oh my God!' Bill Jones came up behind him, staring from Elliot to Hugh's crumpled form.

'Put her in the saddle-room and don't let her out,' Darrow ordered, indicating Beatrix. 'Don't let anyone but me take her away.'

'S . . . sure.'

Darrow didn't even wait to see his orders obeyed, but raced to Hugh's side, cursing himself for his misjudgement of Elliot's temper.

Blood was soaking into the packed dirt of the stable floor beneath Hugh's head. Darrow knelt, knocking Hugh's narrow-brimmed hat aside, and gently turned his deputy's head. More blood matted the golden-brown hair. Darrow wormed one hand under Hugh's muffler, trying to feel a pulse in his neck. He didn't look up as the livery barn door was flung wide open.

'My God! What happened?' Norman stood in the doorway, the tall figure of Josh Turnage beside him as they took in the bloody scene.

The undertaker acted first, joining Darrow at Hugh's side. 'Breathing?'

Hugh was so bundled in his winter coat it was impossible to tell just by looking.

'Yes.' Darrow's face was strained. 'The bullet creased him.'

'Good. I only got one spare coffin right now.' Turnage's actions were softer than his comment as he examined the wound.

Elliot's shot had struck the side of Hugh's head hard enough to knock him unconscious without killing him outright. It was some consolation, but not much yet. Experiences in the Civil War had taught Darrow that head wounds could be tricky things.

'The doc's coming,' said Bramall, the owner of the bathhouse next door.

Darrow and the undertaker covered Hugh carefully with a horse blanket.

'You'd best get him seen to,' Darrow said, indicating Elliot's body.

'Sure.' Turnage spotted his assistant in the growing crowd around the barn door and started giving efficient orders.

Darrow sat back on his heels, one hand resting gently on Hugh's shoulder, and thought of all the people he needed to talk to. He didn't look forward to it.

An hour later, Sheriff Darrow went to visit Beatrix in her cell. Hugh was upstairs, being tended by Doc Travis and his wife. Beatrix had tidied herself up and was sitting on the edge of her bunk, combing her dusky blonde hair and trying to pin it in a new style. She looked up hopefully as Darrow came through the office door, then her face fell and she turned away. Darrow folded his arms and leaned against the lumber wall, watching her silently as she tried to secure a curl above her ear.

Beatrix lost her patience first. 'Haven't you anything better to do?' she snapped.

Darrow raised an eyebrow. 'Haven't you? Or are you expecting another beau to make a noble attempt at rescuing you from my evil clutches?'

'I hate you.' Beatrix turned her back again.

Both of them heard the outside door open, and Henk calling. Darrow answered and Henk came through to join them. He leaned against the steel bars separating him from his pretty sister.

'Beatrix, are you all right?'

Darrow answered first. 'Why she's for sure all right. One man's dead and another's badly hurt, but all she cares about is looking pretty for her beaux.'

'Beatrix could have been hurt this morning,' Henk said, his ruddy face flushed.

'Hugh is hurt,' Darrow returned, the cold humour leaving his eyes. 'Elliot's dead.'

'I never asked him to come rescue me, you know that,' Beatrix said petulantly

Darrow nodded slowly. 'But you did cook up a fake alibi with Bill Jones, didn't you? He's as besotted with you as Elliot was, just less violent.'

'I wish we'd never come to this stupid town,' Beatrix declared, glaring at Henk. 'The men are all fools; they've spoilt everything. I've been miserable since Christmas, all of them whining and demanding that I marry them. As if I wanted to marry a saddler or an engineer.' She shut up suddenly and tossed her head.

Henk was saying soothing things, but Darrow didn't miss the sudden change of subject. He stepped closer to the cell, his dark eyes intense.

'There are no engineers in Govan. The ones who pass through are not here for long enough for you to strike up an acquaintance. Who were you talking about?'

'That's none of your business.'

'It's exactly my business. Your roan mare was tethered near the railroad depot on Christmas Eve, and you knew someone connected with the railroad. Who was it?'

Beatrix bit her lower lip, then turned to her brother for help. 'I thought you were going to get me a lawyer,' she cried, her voice uneven.

'The railroad is blocked by snow; I couldn't get to Laramie,' Henk explained, glancing anxiously at the sheriff.

'I don't want to hear anything about the railroad!' A note of hysteria entered Beatrix's voice. She paused, forcing herself to speak more calmly. 'Send a telegram.'

'I did.'

'Why don't you want to hear about the railroad?' Darrow pressed, his right hand slightly raised as if waiting for something.

Henk intervened. 'Leave her alone, for God's sake. She's just been through a terrifying scene and she's frightened.'

Darrow barely spared him a glance. 'Beatrix, what were you doing at the railroad depot on Christmas Eve?'

'I left!' Beatrix cried, frightened and caught in her own lies. 'I left before Tim did.'

'Ah!' Darrow didn't fail to notice that she'd used a familiar name. 'Tim Judd wanted you to marry him?'

'I couldn't marry a railroad man!' She turned to her brother. 'You wouldn't want me to marry someone like that, would you, Henk?'

'Of course not,' he answered automatically before hesitating. Henk rarely believed anything bad of his adored sister, but he wasn't a fool. Beatrix's reaction warned him that something serious was up. 'You don't have to marry anyone you don't want to, but were you at the railroad depot?' Henk Verstappen was used to ordering other men, but he was no good at being firm with his sister; there was no force in his question.

Darrow had no sympathy for her distress. 'Why, how do you reckon that roan mare caught a chill? She was tethered in trees back of the depot for an hour or more.' Henk studied the sheriff but saw only certainty behind the statement.

Darrow took advantage of their confusion. 'You were visiting Tim Judd right before he was murdered, weren't you?' he asked Beatrix fiercely. 'He wanted to marry you but you weren't interested because you thought you could do better than a railroad depot man; like an English lord, perhaps,' he added, his voice rich with contempt. 'Judd pressed it because he loved you, just like that fool Elliot, and you got mad because you always do when someone crosses you. Right after that, Judd was murdered. Who are you covering for, Beatrix? Who did you steal the gun for?'

'I'm not covering for anyone!' she yelled back, her face flushed. 'You're just lying, you can't prove I did it!'

There was a shocked gasp from Henk. A cold smile touched Darrow's face.

'You didn't have time to run to your

brother for help,' he said. 'Which besotted fool did you get to do your dirty work instead? There had to be one, you'd never do anything for yourself if you could help it,' he needled. 'You're lazy and a coward.'

'I'm not a coward!' Beatrix flung back. She had to tilt her head back to look the sheriff in the eyes, but there was no lack of courage in her angry stance. 'I took care of Judd all by myself!'

'Ah.' Darrow's smile changed to one of satisfaction.

'Beatrix!' Henk exclaimed.

She froze, staring at Darrow and seeing the triumph in his eyes. 'I hate you!' she screamed. 'I hate you! I hate you!' With that she stormed to the back of the cell, dropped on to the bunk and burst into tears.

9

Darrow nodded, satisfied that some good had come from the day's events, and returned to the front office. Henk Verstappen followed, anger and fear both on his broad face.

'You can't prove anything,' he insisted. 'She's hysterical; she doesn't know what she's saying.'

Darrow looked at him calmly. 'Judd was shot with a Smith and Wesson that was stolen from the livery stable that same afternoon. Beatrix was the only visitor to the livery that afternoon.'

Henk grimaced.

'You can't prove she pulled the trigger though.'

Darrow smiled wolfishly. 'Ever wondered how your sister bruised that dainty little hand of hers? Most any gun produces a powerful kick if you don't have hands big enough to hold it properly.'

'Even so . . . ' Henk was running out of arguments. For one thing, he knew how much Beatrix hated to be crossed, and how selfish her temper could be. His businessman's instincts came to the fore. 'Listen, Sheriff, you don't have any real proof that Beatrix killed Tim Judd. Keeping her here has put you to a lot of trouble already. If you turn her over to me, we'll move clear away from Govan. I'd be willing to make it up to you for your trouble.'

A cold look settled on Darrow's face. 'You'd pay me for my trouble?'

Henk nodded, patting the pocket of his jacket. 'All your deputy's doctor bills, and a sum for you.'

'My deputy's name is Hugh Keating. *If* he lives, he's got more than enough money to pay the bills himself.' Darrow spelt it out slowly. 'It's too late to save your sister by bribing me.'

Henk flushed, struggling to control

his temper. 'I wasn't offering to bribe you.'

'It sure sounded like it. I gave my word that I'd bring in whoever killed Tim Judd, and if it's your sister, then it's Beatrix who will stand trial.'

'You'd never get a jury to convict her,' Henk insisted.

'It's a federal case; she'll stand trial in Laramie. I don't think she has any beaux there.'

Henk paced about the office, seething with fury.

His dilemma was interrupted by the arrival of Turnage, the undertaker. Turnage stared thoughtfully at Henk, giving the businessman the feeling he was being measured for his coffin. Henk suppressed a shudder, and spoke.

'I'm riding back to the ranch to speak to Mamma,' he told Darrow. 'I'll come back tomorrow to sort this mess out.'

'You can plan what you like. Beatrix goes to Laramie as soon as the trains are running,' Darrow answered.

'I'll see you in Hell, Sheriff!' Henk

declared as he stormed out.

'How's Hugh?' Turnage asked cheer-fully.

'Doc Travis is still with him,' Darrow answered. 'If you're touting for trade, you're a mite premature.'

Turnage looked offended. 'Even looking on the bright side, Hugh's not gonna be back on his feet for a few days. There's plenty enough folks in town that don't hold with you keeping Miss Beatrix in the hogpen.'

'Like Elliot?'

'He was a touch excitable,' Turnage admitted with masterly understate-ment. 'But I figured that maybe you could use some help.'

'Are you hoping this case will drum up more trade for you?'

Turnage shrugged. 'Ain't no one gettin' buried while the ground's frozen. My customers are getting stacked in the woodshed till it thaws some.'

Darrow couldn't tell how serious the remark was, so he ignored it. He considered the offer of help instead. Josh Turnage would certainly be better at quelling trouble than Hugh had ever been; one look from the lean undertaker was enough to make most people remember business elsewhere.

'All right.' Darrow fetched a Bible from the desk drawer, along with a spare badge, and held them out. 'I'll swear you in as a special deputy.'

Darrow had sworn Josh Turnage in, and was explaining the basic duties, when Doc Travis called him. The sheriff followed him up to the living quarters.

'Hugh's still out,' Doc said succinctly. 'Took a pretty bad knock. Just a matter of wait and see, now.'

They entered Hugh's bedroom, where the doctor's plump wife was watching the unconscious man. Hugh's head was bandaged, and he seemed less white than he had in the stable, but he lay under the heavy quilts with an ominous stillness. Darrow rested his hand on his companion's shoulder, but his stern face showed little.

'All told, I reckon he was lucky,' Doc remarked, packing his black bag.

'There's two men dead now, and one as close as a whisper,' Darrow said, his rich voice strained with anger. 'All because of vanity.' He glanced down at Hugh. 'Beatrix's vanity started this mess for sure, but it's my fault Hugh was standing in front of Elliot.'

'You were only asking him to do his job,' Mrs Travis said soothingly. She bustled up to the sheriff, holding a small ginger kitten that wriggled in her grasp. 'I guess you'd best look after Hugh's pet for him.'

Darrow stared at the kitten with distaste. 'You-all knew about this . . . ?'

'It was sleeping on the quilts when we brought him in,' Mrs Travis answered, stroking it fondly. She thrust the kitten at the sheriff, who took it awkwardly. The ginger kitten immediately set up an ecstatic purring as it gazed at him with great golden eyes. 'It's a dear thing,' Mrs Travis added fondly.

Darrow suppressed his urge to offer her the kitten as a gift. Looking after it would be his penance for getting Hugh hurt. He sighed.

Minnie Davis came to visit later that day. She sat in Hugh's bedroom, talking softly to the bewildered man when he came round. Darrow was grateful for her company as Hugh couldn't remember what had happened at all. Minnie patiently answered the repeated questions, soothing Hugh and telling him how brave he'd been. Darrow viewed Elliot's rescue attempt as a complete fiasco for all parties, and certainly didn't want to admit to Hugh whose gun had been stolen by the saddler. The sheriff stayed in the parlour, watching the kitten chase a scrap of paper about the floor. It tired of its play and jumped on to Darrow's lap, purring as it snuggled against him.

'I reckon I'd better feed you, whatever you're called,' Darrow said. He lifted it carefully to the floor and went to open a can of pressed beef.

The window by the cook-stove looked out over Main Street, facing east. As Darrow chopped the beef fine, he realized the light was fading fast. He leaned forward, peering at the northern sky. A black storm-cloud was brewing there, and the hanging sign outside the Empty Lode opposite was banging back and forth in the rising wind. Darrow dropped the knife and hurried across the room, picking up Minnie's coat and hood as he went. Behind him, the kitten mewed impatiently for its meal.

Minnie looked up as the sheriff appeared in the open bedroom door.

'There's a storm coming fast.' He held the coat out. 'We'd better hustle some.'

Minnie didn't waste words, but quickly said goodbye to Hugh and buttoned herself into her plain navy coat. By the time she had tied her hood on, Darrow was ready too.

'I'll see you back,' he said.

They hurried downstairs and out through the back door. The Davises' house was in the cluster of buildings to the west of Main Street, and the quickest way was through the maze of alleys between them. They trotted along together, not wasting breath on words. The wind was rising fast and Minnie was hampered by her long skirts and the layers of petticoats that pressed against her legs and whipped round.

They had passed two shanties before the storm hit. The light vanished as fast as a lamp being extinguished. A howling wind struck them, scouring their faces with frozen snow. Darrow grabbed for Minnie's arm and hung on to her as she staggered. It was pointless trying to say anything; the storm wind deafened and blinded them.

Darrow bowed his head and kept walking, keeping hold of Minnie with one hand while the other stretched into the darkness. He took a few steps and paused. Darrow knew the maze of passages between these houses better than anyone in town. He should have been able to touch the Browns' house.

He moved sideways, taking half a pace left, and his outstretched fingers made contact. Darrow couldn't see the lumber house in front of him, but he could feel the boards with his fingers.

He moved on more confidently, letting the wall guide him. They were unlikely to wander into open country, as they would hit either the railroad or the river first, but the intense cold of the blizzard was dangerous. Darrow had a knot of ice in his middle already and Minnie was so small and slight she would surely be feeling worse. He moved as briskly as he could, lending his strength to Minnie as she staggered. Her full skirts dragged her about as the wind changed direction. The wind beat against them, smothering them as they struggled against it.

Darrow's hands were going numb, in spite of the thick woollen gloves. Even so, he felt the corner of the Browns' house and knew they must risk a few steps into the white nothingness to reach Minnie Davis's home. He took a good grip of the corner of the Brown building, doing his best to ensure that he was facing straight across the gap separating them from the Davis house. Darrow could visualize the corner in his mind. He set off, trying to count his steps, but the wind pushed him sideways and tried to drag Minnie from him. He knew he'd already taken more than ten paces, but he couldn't feel a building ahead of them.

He kept going, trying to drag the freezing air through his muffler and into his lungs. A few more steps and his outstretched hand cracked painfully against something solid. The cold made the shock of impact worse, but he didn't have the breath to curse the pain. Darrow moved close against the lumber wall and felt his way along until he reached the door. He fumbled at the latch, his cold fingers clumsy as he struggled.

Someone opened the door from the inside; Darrow stumbled through, pulling Minnie after himself. Warm, golden lamplight made them blink as Minnie's mother hurried forward to help them.

'Oh, I'm so glad to see you,' she exclaimed, pulling her daughter towards the stove. 'I was terrified that you were wandering somewhere in town.'

The three young boys all stared at the frozen figures, half-covered in snow.

'We'll make up enough room for you here, Sheriff,' Mr Davis offered.

'I've got to get back to Hugh,' Darrow answered truthfully.

'Stay a little and get warm first,' Mrs Davis insisted kindly.

The warmth of the pretty parlour was tempting; Darrow was shivering and his feet hurt, but he refused politely.

'I'd best go afore the storm gets any worse. Thank you-all for your kindness.'

Mr Davis opened the door for him. 'Thank you for helping Minnie. Take care,' he added sincerely.

Darrow nodded as he headed back into the blizzard.

The storm wind swept around the

buildings, buffeting him so hard it was impossible to walk in a straight line. Darrow tucked one hand in his coat pocket and reached out with the other, feeling his way along buildings when he could. Icy particles of snow scoured against his eyes and face. He could hardly keep his eyes open, let alone see where he was going. There was a deep knot of cold in his middle, which ached and set off waves of shivers through his whole body. Darrow struggled on, struggling to draw the air through his frozen muffler. His chest ached with every breath, his hands and feet had gone numb.

He walked into a building and followed it round, trying to keep track of where he was. The constant buffeting of the changing wind kept trying to take him off track. Darrow fought his way along, going more and more slowly as he began to think that he'd got turned around. He could see no more than occasional glimpses of shadowy buildings, but his sense of direction warned him that something was wrong.

He turned, staggered sideways, and walked on. Each step should be bringing him closer to another building, but there was nothing. Darrow pressed on into the whiteness, until suddenly a wall loomed in front of him. He leaned gratefully against it for a moment, then felt his way along until he reached a window. A plain blind had been drawn down inside, but Darrow recognized it. He was out back of the feed store next to his own home.

Encouraged, he felt his way along, crossed the gap between the buildings, and finally reached the back door of the law building. Again he fumbled at the latch with numb hands until the door swung open and he staggered inside. Darrow forced himself to turn and close the door before he gave up and slumped against the wall, shivering and gasping for breath.

Beatrix glared at him from her cell. She had both blankets wrapped round herself and a shawl over her head.

'I was hoping you'd get lost out there,' she said spitefully.

'In which case, you'd have been stuck in here with no food or water until the blizzard stops,' Darrow retorted. He pushed himself upright and walked stiffly past her to the stairs.

'Wait!' Beatrix called. 'It's freezing down here. You can't make me stay here!'

Darrow didn't even bother answering.

★ ★ ★

In the Bar M ranch house, Whilhelmina Verstappen kept her staff busy by ordering the maids to turn out Beatrix's room. Mrs Verstappen issued a string of brisk orders that kept two maids busy and warm through the blizzard. On the second day of the storm, the younger maid, Trixie, tapped on the parlour door.

'What iz it?' Mrs Verstappen called, looking up from her embroidery.

Trixie entered the warm parlour and bobbed an awkward curtsey. 'I turned the mattress and I found this iron underneath.' She held out a revolver.

Henk took it, passing it to his mother at her curt gesture. Mrs Verstappen turned the gun over, surprised to find out how much it weighed. She knew nothing about guns and certainly couldn't tell the difference between Henk's small Colt and this Smith & Wesson. She looked up and saw the maid watching her expectantly.

'Beatrix feels ze need for some protection in zis wild country,' Mrs Verstappen said firmly. 'Henk bought zis for her.'

'I got it last year,' Henk added, inspired by his mother's quick thinking.

'Where should I put it?' Trixie asked.

'I will look after zis,' Mrs Verstappen answered firmly. 'Zere's no need to tell anyone about it, you understand?' There was steel in her soft voice.

The maid nodded and hurried back to her work.

Mrs Verstappen looked at the dull, unpolished Smith & Wesson, then gave it to Henk. 'Did you buy it?'

He shook his head. 'It's the same as the one stolen from the livery barn.' His normally ruddy face had paled. 'Beatrix must be involved in this mess after all.'

'We will protect her,' Mrs Verstappen said firmly. 'When ze blizzard stops, take ze gun out and lose it somewhere.'

'We have to get Beatrix out and away from here,' Henk said determinedly. 'I'll get some men and ride to town. Elliot couldn't manage on his own, but the deputy's out of the way now.' He began to pace about the room, twisting his signet ring as he thought aloud. 'Judd must have been pestering Beatrix. I bet she was frightened of him; that's why she must have shot him.' Henk grew outraged as he began to believe in the excuses he invented for his sister's actions. 'We'll show Sheriff Darrow that he should have let her alone . . . '

'Not yet,' his mother interrupted. She picked up her embroidery again. 'Ze men will want money, and they could use zis as blackmail against us. As you say, ze deputy is out of ze way. Ze sheriff cannot be everywhere at once.'

Henk drew closer to his mother, listening as she outlined her plan.

10

Sheriff Darrow looked up from the Dickens novel he was reading that evening.

'Would you like a cup of coffee?' Beatrix offered gently. She smiled modestly, her dimples showing briefly. The blizzard was still storming outside, scouring the walls and rattling the windows. It was a bleak and unpromising start to the New Year of 1876. Beatrix had a grey-and-pink-silk shawl draped around her shoulders, and wore light, lacy gloves. She looked dainty and lovely and to Darrow, she looked cold.

'Coffee would be fine,' he answered.

Beatrix smiled in reply and went to clatter around by the stove.

Darrow watched her from the corner of his eye. She had spent the first day of the blizzard snapping at him and largely ignoring Hugh, who was still confined to bed. Then she'd said that she'd been silly and selfish, which Darrow entirely agreed with, and she'd been trying to charm him ever since. The sheriff admitted to himself that she was pretty, graceful and had charming manners when she wanted to use them. Beatrix had a way of looking at a man as if he were the most interesting thing in the world. Darrow sat back and let her run around making his life comfortable.

Beatrix laughed as the ginger kitten played with the flounces on her skirt. She twitched her hips around, making the skirt swish across the floor for the kitten to chase. Darrow left them to it, waiting for the cup of indifferent coffee she was preparing.

He had just found his place in *Bleak House* again when the room fell silent. When he looked up, Beatrix was standing by the stove, looking puzzled. She pulled back the heavy curtain to peer out at the night.

'I can't see anything unusual out there,' she reported. 'Just heavy snow.

Oh! The blizzard's stopped.' She spun round, clapping her hands with delight. 'The blizzard's stopped at last.'

The noise of wind and ice had stopped almost as suddenly as it had started.

Darrow put his book down carefully, and stretched.

'How's the coffee?'

Beatrix glanced at the kettle. 'Another couple of minutes.' She smiled up at the sheriff as he approached her. 'You were right. You said it would probably end today, right for the new year, and you were right.'

'I usually am.' Darrow took her arm. 'I'll finish up the coffee for you.' He started leading her to the stairs. 'Where are you going?' Beatrix exclaimed, hanging back.

'The storm's over; you're going back to your cell.' Darrow's voice was implacable.

'No! Oh, please, Sheriff,' Beatrix added more moderately. 'It's so lonely and dull down there and today's a holiday. I've been trying so hard to be nice to you.' She clung to his arm and peered anxiously up at him, a frail, anxious doll-woman.

'I know.' Darrow smiled wolfishly.

The sweetness vanished in a moment. 'Why, you've been fooling me all along!' Beatrix exclaimed.

'You were trying to fool me,' Darrow said reasonably.

'I hate you!' Beatrix yelled as she was towed along. As they reached the top of the stairs, she tried to sit down and become a dead weight.

Darrow merely turned, and before Beatrix realized what he was doing, he had picked her up and slung her over his shoulder like a sack of grain. She burst into tears, too humiliated even to struggle as he carried her down and dumped her into her cell.

'For shame,' he remarked. 'Crying like a little baby.'

Beatrix sat on her bunk, dishevelled and tear-stained, and glared helplessly at him.

By the next morning the town was full of life as everyone came out to do shopping, visit neighbours or simply to see fresh air and sunshine again. When Minnie Davis arrived to visit Hugh, Darrow left the sheriff's office to stroll around his town. Ice and snow glittered in the brilliant sunshine as the sheriff breathed in the clean, fresh air. He stopped at the railroad office to speak to Appleton, who told him that the railroad was blocked even more solidly than before.

'The snow they dug out last time, all thrown up on the banks of the cutting, y'see? Not ten foot of frozen snow to dig out this time; twenty foot!' Appleton sounded as if he wanted to tackle the lot himself. 'And the snow-plough train got snowed under,' he added with a rich chuckle. 'Got to dig out the train afore they can dig out the cutting.'

'Sounds mighty well-organized,' Darrow remarked drily.

Appleton nodded. 'Sure is. Got a double crew working for double pay.

Trains'll be through next week.'

Darrow was less optimistic. He remembered Hugh's comments about the merchants being low on goods, and decided to do some shopping before doing the rounds of the town. He was sure there would be another blizzard before long, and the sheriff put his comfort before the remote chance of any trouble having occurred during the last storm. Besides, Josh Turnage would be looking after the law office and Darrow had greater faith in the undertaker than he did in his deputy.

★   ★   ★

Henk Verstappen avoided the main route into town, instead approaching Govan through the ford not far back of the livery barn. The two horses were reluctant to enter the river but he encouraged them gently until they broke through the rim of ice edging the water, and splashed across.

Henk was riding his favourite and

was leading Beatrix's bay. The beautiful roan mare had recovered from her chill, but Henk wanted a sturdier and fitter horse today. The river water froze into icicles on the horses' tails as Henk followed the river bank, skirting the smithy and the laundry. A couple of minutes later he dismounted at the back of the sheriff's office. Henk drew his Colt from his waistband and listened at the rear door. Hearing nothing, he tugged the door open and tiptoed in. The two big cells were in this back corridor, with the stairs at the far end from the door. Henk hurried to his sister's cell, gesturing for her to remain quiet. 'Is anyone in the office?' he whispered.

Beatrix pressed eagerly against the barred door.

'No. The sheriff's gone out and Hugh's upstairs with plain old Minnie Davis looking after him.' Henk nodded, his heart thudding with nerves as he entered the office.

The room was silent and chilly in

spite of the sun streaming in through the windows. Henk searched the desk rapidly until he found a bunch of long keys. He gathered them carefully, so they wouldn't rattle, and hurried back to the cells, closing the office door behind himself.

'Hurry up,' Beatrix urged. She had put her coat on and was fastening her feather-trimmed hat over her curls.

'Do you know which is the right one?' Henk spread the keys out.

Beatrix shook her head. 'Just try them all and hurry up about it.'

'Shut up!' Henk snapped at his beloved sister for once. 'I don't want to get caught and locked up as well.' He tried the key, listening to the noises upstairs.

'You've got to get me out,' Beatrix hissed. 'That sheriff's been manhandling me.'

'What!' Henk jerked upright, anger flushing his face.

Beatrix nodded, her face sharp with venom. 'I've never been so humiliated.'

'I'll kill him,' Henk growled. He jerked the uncooperative key from the lock and tried another, straining to turn it. Giving up, he was trying a third one when he heard the unmistakable click of the office door opening behind him.

Henk spun, lifting the Colt awkwardly in his left hand, and found himself staring at Josh Turnage. The undertaker looked at the gun trained on him, then at the bunch of keys hanging from the lock. Henk's heart thundered as he struggled between panic and courage. He simply dithered, anxiety clear on his ruddy face.

'Henk, unlock this door,' Beatrix insisted. 'He's unarmed.'

Turnage ignored her logic, staring with disconcerting calmness at Henk.

'I should arrest you,' he remarked.

'You can't,' Henk answered wildly. 'You're not the sheriff.'

Turnage smiled slowly and pushed back his unfastened overcoat to show the badge pinned to his black jacket.

'All sworn in and legal.'

Henk took a deep breath, wondering what to do. The undertaker wasn't carrying any weapon, but something in his eyes unnerved Henk. There was an unnatural calmness; an acceptance of life and death that made him the master of the situation, not the man with the gun.

'Henk!' Beatrix exclaimed. 'Get me out of here.' She shot a vicious glance at Turnage who ignored her, his attention on her brother.

'I reckon you'd better leave,' the undertaker told Henk, taking a step closer to the gun. 'You go now and I'll not tell the sheriff about this.'

Henk didn't know what to say. He stared at Turnage as if hypnotized.

'Shoot him,' Beatrix exclaimed. As her brother hesitated, she reached through the bars, trying to get the gun herself.

Turnage turned his attention to her.

'Leave that.' His voice came out low and threatening. 'I don't have any fancy coffins in stock at the moment, and I'd hate to see a lady as lovely as you buried in a plain pine box.'

Beatrix hesitated, forgetting that he was unarmed. She met the undertaker's gaze.

Turnage scanned her slowly, his gaze travelling from her dainty shoes to the hat covering her fair ringlets.

'You'd best be leaving,' he repeated to Henk. Henk backed away, leaving the bunch of keys dangling from the lock. Turnage turned to scrutinize him again and Henk backed away faster, not wanting to meet the undertaker's eyes again. Henk reached the back door of the law building and clumsily elbowed it open. Turnage watched him with a silent patience which said that Henk would be coming to him in the end. Henk shoved the door open wide and fled.

Turnage waited a few moments, until he heard the pounding of hoofs on the packed snow outside, then went to close the door. Once beyond Beatrix's line of sight, he permitted himself a silent sigh of relief. He locked the back door and returned to the cells, retrieving the bunch of keys still dangling from the lock.

'Seems like your loving brother thought better of his plan,' he remarked.

Beatrix glared at him as she jerked the strings of her bonnet undone.

'I'm going to scream, and when people come running, I'll tell them you were molesting me.'

Turnage merely raised an eyebrow.

'With your reputation, everyone will think you invited me in.'

Beatrix flushed red. 'I hate you! I hate this whole stupid town. I hope it burns down, with you all in it.'

Turnage laughed. 'And you trapped here in the cells,' he pointed out.

Beatrix turned her back on him and threw herself on to the bunk. Turnage smiled to himself and went to replace the keys in the office drawer.

Whilhelmina Verstappen heard hoofs outside and hurried to the parlour windows, peering out through the layers of lace and flowered curtains. She saw Henk ride round the house to the stable, leading his sister's bay horse. Mrs Verstappen fetched her own shawl and bonnet without calling the maid, and went out through the deep snow to the stable. She met Henk inside, where he was giving instructions to the groom.

'Where's your sister?' Mrs Verstappen demanded imperiously, tilting her head back to stare at her son.

'At the jail,' Henk answered briefly, aware of the groom's presence.

'Are you hurt?' Concern showed suddenly on Mrs Verstappen's face.

'No,' Henk confessed, dreading what he knew would come.

'Zen why haven't you got Beatrix?'

Henk recoiled from the explosion of fury. 'I got caught, Mamma. Well, not caught, but Turnage saw me.'

'Who is zis Turnage?' Mrs Verstappen scowled.

'The undertaker. That is, he's been sworn in as a deputy and he saw me trying to get Beatrix out.' Henk had been brooding over his failure all the way home.

Mrs Verstappen stepped closer to her son. 'Did you shoot him?'

Henk shook his head, humiliated but unable to lie to his mother. 'He didn't have a gun.'

'But you did! Why didn't you kill him?'

'I couldn't, Mamma!' Henk exclaimed, shivering at the memory. 'You don't know what he's like. He just stares at you like he's measuring you for a coffin.'

Mrs Verstappen slapped his face. 'You are a coward! You vere supposed to be helpink your sister and you run away.'

Henk recoiled from his tiny mother.

'I'm not a coward! I will get Beatrix

out.' His face darkened as he remembered that Beatrix had been badly treated. 'I've got to get Beatrix out of there,' he said more calmly. 'I'll hire some men and we'll go teach Darrow one hell of a lesson. Then I'll take Beatrix a long way away from here.'

'We must find a husband for her,' Mrs Verstappen said, taking her son's arm. 'She will be a lot less trouble when she is married.' Mrs Verstappen thought nothing of breaking the law to protect her children, but she wasn't completely blind to Beatrix's faults. The girl had to be married off before she completely ruined herself and damaged the family's reputation.

'No,' Henk insisted. 'I can take care of Beatrix.' He stared in the direction of Govan. 'I'll get her back and I'll look after her.'

Mrs Verstappen heard the note of obsession in Henk's voice and stayed silent.

★　★　★

In spite of what he had promised Henk, Turnage told Darrow of what had happened. The sheriff was furious with himself for leaving the keys where they might be found, and grateful for the undertaker's help.

'If it had been you, you'd have probably ended up saddling Verstappen's horse for him,' the sheriff remarked to his deputy that evening.

Hugh was settled comfortably in the rocking-chair by the parlour heater. He was still shaky, and tired easily, but was recovering well from his injury. 'Maybe I should retire and let you take him on full time,' he answered. 'After all, I don't really need to work for my living,' he added as a deliberate afterthought.

Darrow scowled, his dark eyes flashing. 'You don't need to work, and if you ever needed to use your brain, you're so out of the habit you've surely forgotten how.'

'I'm lucky to still have one,' Hugh retorted, lightly touching his bandage.

That struck at Darrow's conscience.

He turned away, almost falling over the ginger kitten as it scurried past, its tail fluffed out to bottle-brush proportions. Before he could see what had frightened the kitten, a storm wind struck the house with a shriek. The light level dimmed instantly as the third blizzard struck the town.

Hugh leaned forward to turn up the kerosene lamp. Darrow fetched the quilt from Hugh's room and tucked it around the rocking-chair.

'Thanks,' Hugh muttered, his dark eyes wide as he looked at the stovepipes where the wind was howling wildly. 'Did you get any stores in?'

'We'll be all right,' Darrow answered absently, arranging more coal on the heater. 'It's going to be bad on the town if this keeps up though.'

'How do you mean?'

'There hasn't been a train through for nearly a week. Van der Leo was expecting a delivery when the trains stopped so he's plumb nearly out of goods. So long as these blizzards keep up, they can't put the train through, and Hinchcliffe can't feed the whole town from his stock.'

Hugh was silent, thinking things through.

Darrow let him brood for a minute. 'Want some coffee?'

'Please.'

The sheriff grinned wolfishly. 'Then I'll let Miss Beatrix out of that cold cell downstairs, and she can fix us some.'

11

The third blizzard only lasted two days. It faded suddenly at noon, leaving the parlour of the law building dim and quiet.

'Thank God for that,' Hugh said, tugging open the thick curtains to let the sun pour in. 'I wonder if the Freight Car's open; I'm dying for a good drink.'

'But not desperate enough to go out in the blizzard for one,' Darrow answered, gathering up the used dinner plates. He looked at Beatrix. 'You want to go back to your cell right now, or would you like to stay up here another half-hour?'

'I'll go down,' she answered crossly. 'I know you want me to do the dishes and I won't. That hot water's ruining my hands.'

Darrow laughed unsympathetically. Beatrix had tried refusing to do her

163

share of the daily chores during the blizzard, so he had refused to let her have so much as a cup of coffee until she gave in. The sheriff had won out, but Beatrix hadn't forgiven him.

'I'll go out,' Hugh decided. 'See if I can rustle up a game of poker this evening.'

The near freezing air outside took Hugh's breath away. Main Street was becoming impassable from great glittering drifts of snow that were packed solid. The crossroads were entirely blocked with a drift as high as the roof of Hinchcliffe's Groceries. It didn't stop the determined men and women from reaching the store to stock up.

Hugh watched for a moment, then picked his way gingerly along the sidewalk, hanging on to the hitching rails for safety. Only Ming Loo, the Chinese cook, was trying to clear snow, hacking away at the frozen layers on the sidewalk outside Mrs Irvine's Eatery. The other storekeepers let the white folds of snow lie banked up like heavy layers of icing. Hugh scrabbled over the drifts of Main Street, his boots slipping on the packed snow. A disconsolate woman was staring at the closed blinds of Van der Leo's store, and the hand-lettered sign that read 'out of goods'. Hugh lost his balance on the drift and tobogganed down on his back, fetching up against the sidewalk with a crash. He used the hitching rail to pick himself up, wincing as snow got inside his scarf.

'Better get over to Hinchcliffe's,' he suggested, scooping snow from his coat collar.

'I sure hope he's got coffee, baking-powder and flour,' the woman grumbled, setting off. 'I used up most of my stores doing the Christmas baking.'

Hugh picked his way along to the Wells, Fargo office and let himself in.

Whiskers greeted the deputy cheerfully, and offered him a swig from a bottle.

'Thank you.' Hugh swallowed the

cheap whiskey with an ease that belied his mild appearance. 'That's so much better. I drank all my stuff during the first storm.'

'Guess you're doin' all right,' Whiskers remarked, scratching his brindled beard as he drew another rickety chair up to the stove.

'I'm recovering nicely, thank you,' Hugh answered automatically as he sat. At other times he would have taken far more interest in himself but there was something else on his mind. 'How's the town? Have you heard anything from the railroad?'

Whiskers shook his head. 'Ain't hearing nothing. Line's down.'

'The telegraph lines?'

'Deader'n a bull-calf in a pack of wolves.'

Hugh glanced towards the window. 'It won't get mended in a hurry, will it?'

'Not whiles these damned blizzards keep coming, wham, one after next. I reckons we got another couple weeks o' snow yet.'

Hugh helped himself from the bottle again. 'The town's getting low on food.'

Whiskers nodded and retrieved his bottle. 'It's for-sure gonna get worse afore it gets better.'

Hugh stood up. 'If you're going to hog the drink, I'd better get on with the rounds. Are you coming to the Freight Car this evening?'

''Less there's a storm up,' Whiskers agreed.

'I shall see you later then.' Hugh waved and headed back out into the cold street. The thought of whiskey and cards kept his mind off the temperature and almost helped him to forget just how isolated the little town was.

★   ★   ★

The Verstappens' ranch house was even more isolated on the wide-open land. The clusters of trees to the front and side broke the force of the blizzards a little, but the ground was still deep in snow as Henk led two horses from the stable. He glanced once at the clear sky, then checked the cinches and swung aboard the chestnut gelding. It snorted, sending clouds of white breath into the air.

'Come on, Tom.' Henk pressed his heels against the chestnut's sides and they set off at a steady jog with the bay tied to the back of the saddle.

Henk took the horses along the trail towards Govan, finding his way by trees and rock formations. The horses trotted out fast, excited by the wide-open spaces, but Henk gently controlled the chestnut. Laramie was a two-day ride away in good weather. The deep snow would tire the horses as they forged their way through. Henk planned to follow the railroad to Laramie. The tracks themselves would be covered, but the telegraph poles running alongside would guide him all right.

Once in Laramie, he would make contact with Platt, and they would get some men together. Platt was a professional troublemaker, strong and smarter than most of his sort. Henk Verstappen had used his services before, to warn off and threaten a rival jeweller who had opened a competing shop. This time, they would deal with Darrow and the other lawmen.

Henk scowled as he recalled how he'd been intimidated by an unarmed man. Beatrix had seen him back down and fail. He couldn't bear to fail again, no matter what it cost in money or risk. Henk glanced at the sky again, searching for storm clouds. There were none yet. He didn't know how long he would have between blizzards, no more than two days at most. No coward would take the risk he was taking now on this ride. He couldn't be a coward, even if he had backed down from Turnage. Henk relaxed his hold on the reins and let the chestnut run on as he brooded on Sheriff Darrow, and thought of his revenge.

* * *

Hugh Keating edged his way back along the snowy path of Main Street. He had almost reached the crossroads when he had to stop and lean against a hitching rail to regain his breath. The sheer effort of making his way through the snow and ice was making him gasp and shake, telling him he was not yet fully recovered from his injury. A woman hurried from Hinchcliffe's grocery store, letting the door swing behind her. Shouts and crashes could be heard from inside. The woman skidded on the ice and sat down, dropping her goods. A boy who had been sliding up and down on the drifts grabbed a package and made off with it.

'Hey! Stop there!' Hugh found he didn't have the breath to yell properly.

The boy was out of sight in moments, hidden by the huge frozen drift that filled the centre of the crossroads. Hugh left the relative safety of the sidewalk, skidding and sliding over to the woman, who hadn't bothered rising but was scrabbling up her shopping as best she could. Other people were spilling out from Hinchcliffe's. One man grabbed a tin of coffee that had rolled towards the sidewalk and ran away with it. No one tried to stop him.

'Give me those beans!' the woman snapped, grabbing for a package that Hugh had recovered for her.

'I wasn't going to steal them!' he protested.

She ignored him, snatching up the precious food. Hugh gave up and scrabbled over to join the people peering in through the store windows. There was another crash from inside. Hinchcliffe himself came out, looking around wildly.

'Hugh! They're breaking up my store!' he yelled, spotting the deputy.

Hugh had rarely felt less like getting involved. He was cold and shaky and his head was beginning to ache. However, generations of his family had been raised on the motto of doing their duty. He took a deep breath, and stood upright.

'Somebody please tell the sheriff,' he requested.

Hinchcliffe's grocery store was a mess. Barrels, boxes and sacks had been overturned. The floor was littered with broken crackers, scraps of dried fish and drifts of sugar. Flour sprinkled the two men who were fighting amidst the debris. Hugh recognized them as Sos, from Amy Vialla's place, and Kennick, a teamster. Kennick landed a punch on Sos's ear, knocking him back into a half-empty sack of rice.

'I need that cornmeal for my daughters, damnit!' he yelled.

'I got six women to feed,' Sos bellowed, shaking his head.

'My daughters are more important than your whores!'

Hugh intervened.

'Kennick!' he called. 'Break it up now.' He moved forward, unfastening his overcoat so he could get at his Webley if necessary. 'What's this about?' he demanded, sounding more confident than he felt.

Kennick pointed at Sos. 'He wanted to buy up the whole sack of cornmeal, but my wife ran out three days back. I got three daughters to feed and they ain't had nothin' but bread and potatoes for two days.'

'Very nourishing, bread and potatoes,' Hugh remarked tactlessly.

'I want that goddamn cornmeal!' Kennick yelled, rounding on him.

Sos wanted it too. The whorehouse was running as short of food as every other place in town. While Kennick was arguing, Sos picked up an empty wooden box that had once held salted cod. When Kennick turned on Hugh, Sos swung the flat box viciously into Kennick's knees. As Kennick yelled in pain and staggered, Sos lunged forward and cracked the box over his head.

'Hey! Stop that!' Hugh yelled. He impulsively closed on Sos, who promptly swung the wooden box at him. Hugh tried to reverse direction but it smashed into his shoulder. Hugh grabbed the box and hung on. 'Fighting won't help,' he gasped.

They wrestled for a moment, until Hugh's strength suddenly ebbed. Sos wrenched the box away from him, pulling the shorter deputy off balance. Hugh's vision greyed out with an attack of dizziness. Sos crashed the wooden box hard against the side of Hugh's head. The deputy collapsed sideways into a rack of shoes and lay amongst them too sick and dizzy to move. Sos took his chance to escape. He dropped the box and was heading for the door when it crashed open and Darrow arrived.

'Hold it there!' he snapped, aiming his shotgun at Sos.

Sos raised his hands. 'I was going to fetch help,' he pleaded.

'He was going to steal the cornmeal,' Kennick insisted, hobbling towards Hugh.

'Both of you are under arrest,' Darrow told them, his face stern.

Turnage arrived at that moment, clutching a shotgun. 'Good timing,' Darrow said. 'Watch this pair while I check Hugh.'

He knelt down beside his deputy. Hugh's face was white and tense with pain as he lay with his eyes closed.

'Just lie still,' Darrow said, resting one hand on Hugh's shoulder.

'I think I'm gonna be sick,' Hugh whimpered, and he was.

12

The next morning, to everyone's surprise, was also clear and sunny. After breakfast, Darrow let the two shame-faced brawlers out of their cell and spoke to them in the front office. The sheriff told them both in no uncertain terms what he thought of them.

'I spoke with Justice Robinson and he's going to fine you-all for public affray,' Darrow finished.

'I haven't worked since the heavy snow started,' Kennick said anxiously.

'The matter of fines is up to the Justice,' Darrow pointed out. He knew full well that Robinson would use good sense when setting the fines, but wasn't about to tell the two men that. He frowned at them, his dark eyes cold. 'There will not be a court session until after the blizzards cease.'

'Sure thing, Sheriff,' Sos answered,

buttoning his coat. 'But ... ' he hesitated briefly. 'We're not the only folks in town running short of goods.'

Kennick nodded agreement. 'We had to use the children's Christmas candy to sweeten coffee. We don't have any loaf-sugar left after all the Christmas baking was done.' He made a gesture of frustration.

A touch of sympathy showed on Darrow's face.

'Van der Leo's fitting runners to his wagon. Next time we get a break in the weather, he aims to drive to Laramie.'

Both men, the family man and the bouncer at the whorehouse, looked relieved. They left together, chatting about the merchant's plans.

As they left, Josh Turnage arrived.

'Good morning,' said the undertaker brightly. 'How's Hugh?'

'Still complaining about his head,' Darrow answered. 'It makes a change from his complaints about the cold.'

'At least he's well enough to complain,' Turnage remarked, sitting casually in a chair with his legs stretched out. 'And speaking of complainers, how come Henk Verstappen hasn't been by yet?'

Darrow shrugged as he walked past. 'I'd rather he was here. At least I'd know what he is doing.' He took down his overcoat and muffler and started wrapping up.

'Going to set an ambush for him?' Turnage suggested frivolously.

'I aim to ride out that way while the weather holds. I'd like to know what happened to that Smith & Wesson.' Darrow pulled his hat on firmly.

'Watch yourself,' Turnage warned. 'Only you and Henk heard Miss Beatrix there admit she killed Judd. If you're not around to testify against her, there won't be much of a case.'

Darrow nodded. 'I'll surely take care. And take a shotgun with you when you do the rounds. For sure there's going to be more trouble over food.'

'All right.'

Darrow reached the warmth and

peace of the livery barn without seeing any trouble. Norman was in the saddle-room, cleaning harness. He was surprised to see the sheriff taking his saddle off its stand.

'Don't go too far,' he warned. 'There'll be a blizzard soon, like as not. If you get lost and Hugh's sick, there'll be no one to look after poor Miss Beatrix.'

'Most of the men in town want to look after that Venus fly-trap in skirts,' Darrow retorted. 'If they had to spend three days cooped up, listening to her talking about herself and her clothes, they'd surely change their minds.'

'Miss Beatrix doesn't mean any harm,' Norman protested.

'Her conversation is nearly as deadly as her gun,' Darrow said ungallantly. He wasted no time in saddling the black gelding and riding away from Govan.

The sheriff's ill temper eased as they ploughed along the trail. The black gelding fought its way through the loose snow piled knee-deep over the layers frozen below. Darrow hadn't travelled far when he saw the marks where someone else had broken tracks through the snow recently. He reined in, letting the black gelding blow clouds of hot breath as he examined the marks. Another horse had passed this way recently. The edges of the marks were blurred slightly and were printed over here and there with fresher bird tracks. Someone had ridden from the direction of the Verstappens ranch towards Govan, but had skirted the town and travelled east, towards Laramie.

Darrow looked back at the crumpled snow where his own horse had broken its path. He weighed up the dangers of leaving an obvious trail against the risk of getting lost if he tried to cut across country. Darrow wasn't afraid of Henk Verstappen, but his brief experience in the blizzard with Minnie warned him of what to expect if he were caught in the open. He glanced involuntarily at the northern sky; it was still clear and blue.

Sheriff Darrow urged his horse on again, staying on the trail.

It took him over two hours to make the ride to the ranch, even with the advantage of using the path that the other rider had broken. He had to stop now and again to clear balled snow from the gelding's hoofs, and he stopped once to clear freezing ice from the horse's breath off its muzzle. By the time the ranch came in sight, Darrow was cold inside and his face was sore where the damp ice of his own breath froze into his muffler and rubbed.

He swung off the main trail, keeping the small cluster of trees between himself and the buildings. The trees were mostly bare, branches weighed down with snow, but they were better than no cover at all. As he reined in, Darrow could hear men calling to one another in the yard back of the ranch house.

He dismounted, sinking to his knees in snow, and tethered his black so it wouldn't wander in search of food.

Darrow picked his way between the trees, his black overcoat blending with the grey-brown shadows. He stopped near the edge of the copse, standing behind scrub oak to watch the ranch. The ranch house itself seemed quiet apart from the smoke trailing from the stovepipes. The curtains were half-drawn but there was no gleam of lamplight from within. Darrow stuffed his cold hands deep into his pockets and calculated his chances of getting inside unnoticed. Probably not good, since there were the maids as well as Mrs Verstappen.

Darrow tried to imagine what Beatrix had done with the Smith & Wesson after shooting Judd. He had already searched the copse where the roan mare had been tethered. Beatrix hadn't thought about getting found out and caught; she'd made no plans for the possibility. No doubt she had brought the gun home, to where she felt safe, and had left it there. The best evidence against her was probably in her bedroom, where he couldn't get at it without a warrant from Justice Robinson. Darrow sighed, his breath clouding damply around his face. He gazed around the ranch again, assessing the other buildings as possible hiding places for the gun. At this time of the year, the low sun cast blue shadows over the snow, picking out every little ridge and hollow.

Those shadows showed up a shallow trail in the snow, leading from the ranch house to the copse where the sheriff was standing. Fresh snow softened the broken trail, but the shadows still traced the path. Darrow hurried through the trees to the point where the snow path reached the copse. The trees had broken the force of the blizzard, and protected the footprints better. The sheriff had no difficulty following the tracks to a willow tree, where the snow had once been disturbed. Darrow crouched down and started digging, using his pocket knife and his gloved fingers to scrape away the packed snow.

He didn't have to dig far before he found something wrapped in flowered fabric. The sheriff chipped away snow and ice eagerly until the package came loose. The cloth was stiff with cold but he prised it open to reveal the Smith & Wesson revolver.

The sheriff gazed at the gun with satisfaction, then swiftly wrapped it again. He looked at the quiet ranch house, and a wolfish smile showed on his face as he studied the flowered pattern of the parlour curtains and compared it to the piece he held. He returned to the black gelding and put the wrapped gun into his saddlebag.

'A pretty satisfying trip, Gabriel,' he told the horse, rubbing its ears. The gelding snorted and shook its head. Darrow mounted gracefully, letting his coat skirts hang over the back of the deep saddle. 'Let's get home and warm.'

The journey back seemed even longer than the trip out. They could follow their own trail but the gelding was still up to his knees in broken snow. The horse was soon sweating in spite of the intense cold. Darrow tried walking and leading his horse, but it meant he had to walk in the unbroken snow, which was slow and tiring. He soon mounted again, pausing to scrape balled snow from his horse's hoofs first. The winter sun was getting low in the sky when the town finally came in sight. Darrow was aching with cold and hunger, and the black horse plodded steadily on with its head low. Darrow was jolted from his numbness by a gust of icy wind that tore at his hat. He turned instinctively to the northern sky, and saw the black storm cloud move up to drown the weak sun.

'Get a move on there, Gabriel,' he urged swinging the reins against the horse's neck. The startled gelding stumbled into a jog, slipping now and again in the snow. Darrow hated to push his unwilling, tired horse, but they were racing a blizzard.

He made it to the livery barn with a

few minutes to spare. Luckily Norman was still at his barn and he took the weary horse from the sheriff.

'Look after him well,' Darrow ordered, taking the fabric bundle from his saddlebag. 'He's helped me catch a murderer.'

Darrow hurried back to his office, where he found Josh Turnage pacing anxiously. The undertaker smiled with relief as the sheriff returned.

'I was thinking you'd get caught out there,' he said, snatching up his own hat and coat.

'Any trouble in town?' Darrow asked, gratefully unwinding his muffler.

'Only when that Queenie came by to say hello to Hugh,' Turnage said. 'Trouble was, Minnie Davis was here already. You never saw two women be so gosh-damned polite to one another.'

'Neither of them will be visiting for the next day or two,' Darrow remarked.

He saw the undertaker to the door. Both men glanced up at the darkening sky as the storm cloud raced closer. The wind already carried shards of ice.

'I sure pity anyone caught out in that. Even if it is good business,' Turnage said.

Darrow nodded, wondering where Henk Verstappen was.

★   ★   ★

Henk was still in open country when the blizzard hit. His horses noticed the change in the weather before their cold, tired rider. The stocky bay laid back its ears and broke into a jog for a few strides, waking Henk from his light doze. He instinctively tightened the reins, slowing the horse, as he blinked himself awake.

'We're not there yet,' he muttered to the horses, his voice muffled by the woollen scarf over his face. Henk's face was sore, rubbed by the damp scarf, and his eyes hurt from snow glare. As he blinked, he realized that the strong light had gone.

Dawning fear knotted Henk's stomach as he twisted in the saddle to see the black clouds blotting out the sky behind them.

'God, no,' he exclaimed.

The blizzard winds picked up loose snow and flung it into his face. Henk hunched deep into his saddle and urged the horses on. They crabbed along, heads tucked close against their chests and ears laid flat. Then the full storm wind hit man and horses.

Henk knew he wasn't far from Laramie. He'd been checking his course against the snowed-up railroad tracks regularly, and he knew roughly where he was. Henk clutched the reins in one numb hand, pushed the other hand deeper into his coat pocket, and prepared himself to ride out the storm. The blizzard darkened the sky so he couldn't tell how much time was passing. The knot of cold and hunger in his stomach grew increasingly intense, then faded slowly. Henk barely noticed the warning signs, sitting loosely on his horse with his eyes closed against the screaming, scratching wind. The horses plodded on of their own accord. All Henk was aware of was the warmth and sleepiness that slowly crept over him.

The unguided, tired horse stumbled. Henk spilled loosely into the snow, the impact stirring him to vague consciousness. The snow was comfortable and the hollow of his impact sheltered him from the fierce wind. Henk relaxed, he could get to Laramie tomorrow. They could ride back for Beatrix later. The memory of his sister stirred Henk's conscience. He couldn't fall asleep while she was waiting for him to fetch help. Beatrix was relying on him to get her away from Darrow.

Henk suddenly jerked to full consciousness. He floundered in the drift, fear giving him the strength to fight off the deadly sleepiness. Finally getting to his feet, he peered anxiously into the storm for the horses.

'Woody! Tom!' he bellowed hopelessly into the blizzard. Henk stumbled forward, reaching blindly into the storm. A dark shape became visible and he grabbed for it. The chestnut gelding didn't move but stayed with its head low as Henk pulled himself closer to the warmth of its body. The chestnut stayed motionless, its flanks barely moving.

Henk took the stiff reins and looked at the horse's head. The horse's mane, eyelashes and whiskers were coated in ice; more white was frozen over its nostrils and mouth. The horse was smothering under its ice load. Henk laid his hands on its muzzle, letting his own slight warmth soften the ice so he could scrape it away. The chestnut suddenly threw up its head, wild-eyed as it drew a deep breath at last. Henk rubbed its ears between his hands, then followed the lead rope that tethered the horses together to tend the bay too.

As he moved round the bay's head, Henk's shoulder hit against something. He helped his horse first, then reached around behind himself and touched a lumber wall. Henk gave a silent prayer of thanks as he followed the wall around and found himself by a raised sidewalk. The horses plodded after him as Henk began to hurry. He led them to the rear of the building and found the barn. Henk fumbled impatiently with the door, shouldering it open. He stumbled wearily in, blinking at the warm lamplight inside. A man appeared from a stall and stared, still clutching a hoofpick.

'Where in hell did you come from?' he exclaimed, hurrying to close the door behind Henk and the two horses.

'Hell's about right,' Henk answered, stumbling over nothing.

'I'll see to them.' Henk let the man take the horses and staggered to a bale of hay. He sat heavily and watched as the man tended his horses, too tired even to speak. It didn't matter though. He'd made Laramie, and tomorrow he could get men to help him free Beatrix and deal with Sheriff Darrow.

13

The jailhouse was greyish and dim with the curtains drawn against the blizzard outside. It was the longest storm yet; three days now without stopping. Hugh and Darrow were sitting by the chessboard, supposedly playing a game, but the wearying round of storm-trapped days had dulled everyone's senses. Beatrix no longer bothered trying to get their attention. She drifted around the room, wrapped in her shawl, lifting the curtains now and again to stare into the whirling snow. Only the ginger kitten, now named Homer because of his odyssey in the snow, seemed at peace. It slept on Darrow's lap, purring in its dreams.

The sheriff leaned forward, careful not to squash the kitten, and moved an ebony knight. Hugh stared at it, trying to make himself think. The game had dragged on for as long as the storm. Beatrix took no notice of either man, but drifted around the room like a ghost. It was an effort for anyone to even cook food at noon and at suppertime. No one was very hungry except for the kitten. Hugh watched it as it eagerly licked up scrambled egg from a tin plate.

'I'm glad Minnie likes cats,' he said suddenly into the silence. Neither of the other two answered. Beatrix huddled her shawl more tightly around herself, too numb even to feel jealous. They were all just waiting for the storm to end and let them take up their lives again.

★   ★   ★

The blizzard faded away in the night, leaving silence behind. Sunshine glittered in through the storm-dirty windows, bringing life back to Govan. Darrow wouldn't let Hugh linger over breakfast in the sunny room, but hurried him along.

'What's all the rush?' Hugh complained, trailing downstairs after the sheriff.

'People will be out to buy food, and there isn't much left,' Darrow answered curtly. He picked two shotguns off the rack and tossed one to Hugh, who nearly missed it. There was a sharp tap on the door and Josh Turnage entered, also carrying a shotgun.

'Loaded for bear,' he remarked, indicating his gun. 'Or at least hungry mobs.'

Darrow was pleased to see his special deputy, even if Turnage's ability to show up at just the right moment was getting unnerving. The sheriff outlined his plans, then left through the back door as the other two took the front.

The sheriff's office was next door to Hinchcliffe's Groceries, for which Hugh at least was grateful as they forced their way through the knee-deep snow on the sidewalk.

'Gosh! Look at that!' he exclaimed,

pointing to the Empty Lode saloon on the opposite corner. In fact he was pointing to a huge snowdrift that almost completely obscured the two-storey building.

'I bet that's the warmest building in town,' Turnage answered. The frozen snowbank at the crossroads had grown too. The grocery store was on the south-west corner; the funeral parlour was diagonally opposite at the north-east, but couldn't be seen from the deputies' position in front of Hinch-cliffe's.

Hugh stepped into the grocery store to pass on the sheriff's orders, then joined Turnage outside as the first hopeful customers arrived.

'The store's closed until further notice,' Turnage was explaining to two men.

'Why's that?' one demanded truculently.

'I want some coffee, damnit,' the other said. 'I know there's some in there.'

'The sheriff's calling a town meeting,' Hugh announced, pitching his voice to be heard by the other people picking their way through the snow to the store.

'I don't want a town meeting, I want food!'

'I want my coffee!'

'Do us a favour, eh, pet?' Queenie asked, pushing her way forward. Hugh and Turnage stood side by side in front of the grocery's door, shotguns held loosely. A mob of townsfolk, men and women, gathered before them. Children ran around, pitching snowballs at one another and sliding on the massive drift. Their joyful shrieks made a shrill counterpoint to the angry voices of the adults.

Weber, the blacksmith, made his way to the front of the crowd. 'We need more food,' he insisted, his German accent sharp.

Hugh shifted his weight uneasily as he defied the massively built man. 'I can't let you in there. Sheriff Darrow's ordered.'

'The sheriff doesn't have the right to close the shops,' Queenie said. Her eyes flirted boldly with Hugh, making him blush.

Turnage answered her calmly. 'The sheriff has special powers in emergencies. Like the power to deputize me. I can now legally shoot you, as well as burying you,' he went on, his voice suddenly as chilly as the snow.

Hugh shivered at the implied threat, grateful that Turnage was on his side.

Weber spoke again, addressing the Englishman directly. 'Ve need food, Deputy Keating. Our baby, she iz hungry.'

'My kids ain't seen nothing but bread and potatoes for a week,' someone else called.

'All the girls are hungry,' Queenie pleaded, genuine need creeping into her voice.

'You will all get food,' Hugh promised anxiously.

Turnage was about to speak when a crash of breaking glass from the back of the store interrupted him. 'Someone's going in the back way,' he said quietly. A few people moved away to see what the noise was. Angry quarrelling could be heard from the back of the store building. The deputies were caught in a dilemma. If they moved to deal with the break-in, the mob would enter the front of the building.

'We can't split up,' Hugh whispered. 'One man couldn't stop this lot.'

Turnage acted first, lifting his shotgun to point it over the heads of the crowd; Hugh belatedly echoed his action.

'No one moves anywhere,' Turnage called. 'We all wait right here until Sheriff Darrow arrives and calls that meeting.'

'They won't shoot unarmed folk,' someone called from the safety of the mass. A snowball flew from the crowd, missing Hugh by inches to splatter against the store. Hugh flinched from the spray of snow.

'It can't hurt you,' Turnage murmured, never taking his steely gaze from the crowd. Three snowballs were flung. One missed, one hit Hugh's shoulder and the third struck Turnage on the side of his face. The undertaker gasped as hidden ice cut his cheek. Blood mingled with the snow on his coat. Hugh ducked as another snowball was flung at them. The front of the mob surged closer.

'That's enough!' Turnage roared, firing into the huge drift. Buckshot kicked up loose snow and shards of ice, showering the angry crowd.

The disturbance at the back of the store was getting louder. Hugh spotted a couple of men making their way to join in and fired over their heads. One man instinctively threw himself down and disappeared into soft snow. His companion left him floundering and hurried on to join the break-in.

'They've only got one shot left each,' someone called.

Turnage pointed his shotgun straight

at the blacksmith. 'My shot will go straight into Weber. If anyone makes a move, they get Weber killed.'

A brief hush fell on the crowd. No one would have believed Hugh, but they didn't know what to make of their undertaker showing such authority.

'You can't let him do that, Hugh, pet,' Queenie called.

Hugh didn't know what he should do.

'I can let him do that,' Darrow answered. The sheriff had come around the other side of the huge drift and was standing on Main Street, his shotgun in his hands. Justice Robinson and Parson Hermann were alongside him.

Robinson moved forward to speak. 'There will be a town meeting in the church at eleven this morning. We will pool all the food in town, from the stores, the Eating House and the saloons, and it will be rationed out among everyone.'

There was a silence as the message sank in. Turnage lowered his shotgun and dabbed at his sluggishly bleeding cheek. The blood was already congealing in the cold air.

'Go round and break up the trouble at the back,' Darrow told Hugh. His courage restored by the sheriff's presence, Hugh obeyed with unusual efficiency.

Darrow stepped onto the sidewalk to join Turnage in front of the store. He surveyed the crowd, his dark eyes picking out each person in turn.

'Go home now,' he told them. 'Make a list of what food you-all have, and bring it to the meeting.'

'Tell your neighbours,' Parson Hermann added, more kindly. 'We must work together at this difficult time.'

'I'm not aiming to arrest anyone now,' Darrow said. 'But this is your last warning. If anyone steals food, or gets into a fight over food, they'll spend the rest of the winter in jail. And believe me, starving is better than eating Hugh's cooking.'

A ripple of laughter passed through

the crowd. The mob was already breaking up, individuals drifting away to get home and check on their supplies for the meeting. Hugh reappeared, looking pleased with himself.

'There you are,' Darrow said ungraciously. 'Go and reckon up the supplies at the jailhouse.'

Hugh's face fell.

The sheriff smiled wolfishly. 'What's the matter? I would have thought that counting tins would suit you perfectly. After all, food doesn't fight back.'

Hugh gave him a wounded look. 'Not unless you've been cooking it.'

* ★ *

By mid-morning, Henk Verstappen had tracked down Platt and his men at one of the larger saloons in Laramie. Henk bought a round of drinks and sat down to outline his problem. Platt leaned back in his chair, sipping at the good whiskey, as he listened. The leader of the gang was a powerfully built man, taller than he seemed at first. He dressed like a dandy, with a brocade waistcoat and a tailored jacket, and kept his black beard neatly trimmed. The gunbelt seemed out of place at first, until a closer look revealed the calculating intelligence in his eyes and the sheer power of his physical presence.

'Sounds like your lil' sister's sure got herself into a mess,' he remarked.

'There's only three men at the jailhouse,' Henk replied. 'One's a useless English nob. The other deputy's the town undertaker.' He managed to sound scornful, even though the thought of Josh Turnage's cold gaze still made him shudder. 'I can't handle all three myself, but with you four it shouldn't be too much trouble.'

Platt leaned forward. 'Except that we're here in Laramie, and your sister's in Govan.'

'You can ride out. I made it here all right.'

Platt shook his head. 'Too damn risky.'

McDermott, on the other side of the table, looked up from the pack of cards he was slowly shuffling.

'That's a hell of a ride in this weather.'

Henk had expected resistance but was too impatient for bargaining; he simply doubled his first offer.

'I'll pay each of you twice the usual rate.'

Platt noticed the quick suggestion but it didn't change his mind.

'Sorry, Verstappen. This is blizzard weather, and no cash money can help iffen you get caught out. A man'd have to be plumb foolish to try.'

His three men nodded and agreed. McDermott was loudest in his agreement; he liked his comforts and an easy life. Perry just gave his boyish smile, willing to go along with whatever Platt thought was good. Campbell, the shortest man, hitched his thumbs into his double gunbelt and waited silently.

Henk ignored those three, knowing it was Platt he had to convince.

'All right. I'll pay you three times the usual.'

Perry gave an appreciative whistle. 'I can stand getting a little cold for that much *dinero*. I say we go.'

'You don't boss this show,' Platt reminded him.

'No, but three hundred dollars. We could sit out the rest of the winter pretty good on that much,' Perry insisted, smiling brightly. He leaned closer to his boss. 'Say yes.'

Platt grabbed the front of the youth's shirt before anyone knew what was happening. He dragged the youngster down so their faces were a few inches apart.

'Iffen I want to hear you speak, I'll ask for it. Otherwise keep your hole shut.' He thrust the youngster away with contemptuous strength, almost throwing him to the floor. Perry recovered his balance and moved away; the smile suddenly gone from his face.

'It isn't the money,' Platt explained to

Henk. 'We got cash enough right now.'

'Hellfire, we can just tap someone in the street,' added Perry, regaining his nerve. He looked like a cheery farm-boy, but he had no conscience at all.

Frustration welled up inside Henk. He fidgeted with his signet-ring, twirling it round his finger.

'God damn you!' he exclaimed. 'Beatrix is in jail, don't you understand! That sheriff's got her locked up; God only knows what he's doing to her. My sister's going to stay locked away like a common whore unless I can get her out of there!'

Platt was unmoved. 'I don't care much for tangling direct with the law, and I'm not leaving town until the blizzards stop.'

'Damn you for a coward!' Henk yelled. He grabbed his glass and swallowed the remains of his whiskey.

'There's nothing cowardly about having the good sense not to get caught in a blizzard,' Platt answered, his voice low and dangerous.

Henk was beyond caring whom he offended.

'I'm a businessman, not a rough-neck or a range hand like you. I still rode two days through that goddamned snow to get to Laramie because I thought you'd have the guts to ride out there and help me get my sister back. I rode through a blizzard to find you, and now you sit here in this saloon and tell me you don't like tangling with the law, and you can't face some snow. I came to you because you're the best in this town, Platt, and I thought you could do the job. Well, I'll go find someone who does want to earn some money. I'll pay whatever I have to, but I'm going to get someone to help me get Beatrix back.' He thumped the solid card table.

'I am the best in this town,' Platt said coldly.

'We're the best,' corrected Campbell, who was always ready to feel overlooked. Platt and Henk Verstappen ignored him, facing each other across the table.

Platt stood up suddenly. 'We'll prove we're the best by making this goddamn stupid ride to get your sister out. If we're going, we'll go now, and you'd better pray for two clear days between storms.' He nodded to his men. 'Come on.'

Henk followed, too anxious for his sister to worry much about blizzards.

14

The weather remained still and silent, with barely a breeze to break the hush. The deep snow was crisp and frozen underfoot. High drifts piled up against the lumber houses, insulating them and keeping them warmer than at any time since the blizzards started. In the jailhouse, Darrow ordered that Beatrix was to remain in her cell. He spoke to Hugh and Turnage in the office.

'Someone rode out to Laramie before the last blizzard. The only reason that I can think of why Henk hasn't visited recently, is that he's surely planning something.'

Hugh nodded wisely. 'He's gone to get that lawyer he threatened us with.'

Darrow withered him with a look.

'Don't be any more stupid than you have to. A lawyer couldn't do anything until the blizzards cease and court sessions start again. Henk wouldn't risk his life riding to Laramie just to wait around with a lawyer. He's gone to get himself some gunmen.' He looked at the undertaker. 'You swore to help out round this one-horse town while Hugh was injured, and I'm mighty grateful. Now Henk Verstappen could be here later today or tomorrow, with armed men. I'll let you go from your post if you want.'

Turnage smiled as he lifted his shotgun.

'I wasn't expecting this kind of trouble when I offered to help,' he admitted. 'But I guess I'll stick around and bag myself some more trade.' He caressed the barrels of the shotgun.

Darrow looked disconcerted for a moment, then shuttered his expression.

'Good. Now, Henk Verstappen can't be here before late afternoon. Until then we'll do the rounds as usual. As soon as it starts going dark, you-all return here. We're going to keep some good solid walls between ourselves and

Henk Verstappen.'

'And let's hope he gets caught in a blizzard somewhere,' Hugh finished.

The midwinter sun was setting when Henk Verstappen, Platt and his men rode into Govan. Hugh's wish for a blizzard hadn't been answered; the day had remained eerily still. Henk wanted to go straight to the sheriff's office, but Platt refused.

'You want me to get into a tangle with the sheriff when I'm so cold I can't hardly hold my reins?' he snapped, hunched deep into his saddle. 'Get some sense in you.'

'Goddamn it, I want to get warm,' McDermott whined.

Henk glowered at the gunmen. He, too, was cold and exhausted from the difficult ride, but his anxiety for his sister drove him on.

'We should move now, before there's another blizzard,' he insisted. Platt turned his horse towards the welcoming sign of Pinder's hotel.

'If there's a blizzard tonight, your

sweet lil' sister won't be going anyplace. She'll still be at the jailhouse when it stops.'

Henk hauled his horse around by the reins, barging it into Platt's mount. The startled horses whinnied as they skidded on the frozen snow.

'Don't you speak of my sister in that way!' Henk yelled.

Platt snarled, his powerful body full of suppressed menace.

'Don't forget who you're talking to, Verstappen. Don't you try shoving me around.'

'Not if you want to keep your balls attached to your body,' hissed Campbell, the short man, his hand resting on the butt of his right Colt.

Henk glared at the gunmen; even McDermott had his coat unfastened and looked ready for action.

'I didn't mean that,' he backed down reluctantly.

'Turning yellow?' Campbell taunted, showing his teeth in a rare smile.

'I'm just anxious about Beatrix,'

Henk explained grudgingly.

Platt had had enough. 'Let's get the damn horses settled and get inside,' he ordered. 'I want some coffee.'

'All right. We can get some food and plan things. We need to get the sheriff out of that office,' Henk said.

Platt grinned suddenly. 'I've got an idea about that,' he promised.

★ ★ ★

Miraculously, no blizzard started during the night. Beatrix picked up on the undercurrent of tension in the sheriff's office when Hugh brought her some breakfast.

'What's the matter?' she asked snappily as she took the bowl of porridge. 'Sheriff Darrow been bullying you again?'

'Not bullying,' Hugh answered gloomily, closing the cell door again and locking it. 'He's worried that your brother's going to try something foolish.'

Beatrix's face lit up. 'Henk's coming for me? Oh, I knew he would.'

Hugh scowled. 'If he does, it's going to be awfully messy. Darrow won't just let you go, you know. He gave his word that he'd bring Tim's killer to justice.'

Beatrix started absently twirling a ringlet around her finger.

'I'd hate to see you get hurt,' she said, opening her green eyes wider. 'You got hurt already because of me.'

'Hurt?' Hugh exclaimed. 'That hulking great fool, Elliot, nearly killed me.' He touched the scar on the side of his head.

'It was awful,' Beatrix sympathized. 'I cried and cried.'

Hugh's vanity got the better of him. 'You did?' he asked, smiling a little. Beatrix nodded, giving the impression of being overwhelmed by emotion.

'It can't have been a nice thing for a lady to see,' Hugh said kindly.

'I do hope nothing like that will happen again,' Beatrix said.

Hugh lost his smile. 'Darrow never breaks his word.'

'And Henk will do anything to get me free,' Beatrix told him. She let him think about that for a few moments, then her face lit up. 'I know!'

'You think you can talk your brother out of fighting?' Hugh asked.

Beatrix shook her head impatiently. 'I know what we've got to do to stop the fight before it even starts.'

'What?' Hugh asked eagerly.

Beatrix smiled at him. 'You can do it, Hugh. If you let me go now, I'll find Henk and we'll go right away from here. There'll be no more trouble and no shooting.' She reached through the bars to hold his arm. 'Just think, Hugh, nobody would get hurt.'

His free hand moved to the pocket where the keys were, then stopped.

'I'd get hurt, by Darrow.'

Beatrix swallowed her impatience and continued pleading with him. 'Hugh, please, do this for me. Darrow won't shoot you, after all.'

'But I might wish he would,' Hugh answered.

His voice was firm but Beatrix could see hesitation in his soft, brown eyes as he looked at her. She pulled his hand through the bars and gently kissed the palm.

'You're a gentleman,' she said quietly, letting tears well up in her eyes. 'I couldn't bear to be locked away in a horrible cold jail. They'd cut all my hair off. Please help me, on your honour as a gentleman.' She kissed his hand again.

Hugh's vivid imagination saw the picture she described and his soft heart was touched. However, he swallowed, then detached his hand from her grip and moved away.

'You're very lovely,' he said quietly. 'But you've overlooked something. Tim Judd was one of my best friends, and you shot him. I won't let you go.'

Beatrix gave a moan and reached for his hand again, but Hugh backed away.

'Oh, please,' she called.

Hugh merely looked at her, an

216

unusual stubbornness on his mild face. 'No.'

Beatrix cried more, this time with real tears of disappointment. Darrow could have told her not to bother; when Hugh made up his mind to something, he was as stubborn as an army mule. Hugh sternly turned his back on Beatrix and walked away.

★　★　★

'No rounds this morning then?' Turnage asked. The undertaker turned a chair round and sat on it the wrong way, leaning his arms on the back.

'We'll wait in here,' Darrow ordered, trying to ignore the undertaker's casual pose even though it grated on his sense of dignity.

Hugh spoke up. 'If Verstappen got caught in a blizzard on his way to Laramie, we could be stuck in here a long time,' he complained, glancing around the office.

'It would make our lives too easy if

217

he had,' Darrow answered, a ghost of a smile touching his face. 'And since when was your life too easy?'

Hugh grunted acknowledgement and checked his Webley yet again.

Josh Turnage studied the Englishman with interest. 'Bill Jones told me you were born with a silver spoon in your mouth,' he remarked.

'Well, yes,' Hugh admitted. 'The Keatings do own large estates.'

'Then what in hell are you doing out here?'

'Gambling,' Hugh answered succinctly. 'First my father thought I was going to gamble my inheritance away in the clubs, then I was much better than he'd expected and he got worried in case I was cheating.'

'Which would be worse?' Turnage was getting interested.

'Oh, cheating,' Hugh answered instantly. 'Well, gambling away fortunes has gone out of fashion rather; they used to do it all the time in the last century. But for a gentleman to get caught cheating would never be forgivable.'

'I guess that you'd have to be good enough that they'd never catch you.'

Hugh smiled. 'I am. But Father insisted . . . '

The rest of the story was lost in the shattering of glass as something was hurled through the window of the law office.

All three men cringed away from the window as glass flew. Something wrapped in dark-blue cloth bounced and rolled on the floor, fetching up against the side of the desk. Cold wind gusted in through the jagged hole in the glass. Darrow flattened himself against the wall and peered cautiously through the window at an angle.

'I can't see anyone,' he reported.

Turnage picked up the bundle and unwrapped it. 'Looks like a woman's hood,' he said, finding a snowball and a piece of paper in the middle of the cloth.

Hugh snatched it from him. 'I think

it's Minnie's.' He fell silent.

Darrow cursed quietly and took the note that Turnage showed him. The sheriff scanned the paper quickly.

'Verstappen wants us to bring Beatrix to the lumber-yard. He says he'll do the swap there.'

'Do you think he'll release Miss Davis all right?' Turnage asked Darrow.

'He'd better!' Hugh exclaimed, genuinely angry. 'This is nothing to do with Minnie. How dare he use her like this!'

'Go upstairs and see if anyone's watching this place,' Darrow ordered him.

When Hugh came down again, both Darrow and Turnage were wrapped up for going outside, and were carrying long guns.

'There was a stranger over by Elliot's shop,' Hugh reported. 'A small chap wearing two pistols. He wasn't at the food meeting.'

'No one would travel out here without a plumb good reason,' Darrow said. 'He'll be with Henk Verstappen for

220

sure. Was there anyone out back?'

Hugh shook his head. 'Couldn't see anyone.'

Darrow made his plans while Hugh got ready. 'We'll take Beatrix out down Main Street, then cut between the feed-store and the Freight Car to cross the railroad to the lumber-yard. Turnage, you leave through the back door, and try to keep out of sight.'

'Right,' the undertaker nodded.

* * *

The Main Street of Govan was surprisingly quiet when Hugh, Darrow and Beatrix set out. All the food in town had been distributed at the church meeting, so no one needed to go shopping. Housewives had done their washing the day before and were ironing today. A few men had gathered in the warmth of the saloons for a social drink, but the street was deserted aside from the children playing on the giant drift at the crossroads. Darrow led the way, his Winchester in his arms. Hugh followed, holding Beatrix Verstappen firmly by her right arm. If she had entertained any thoughts about breaking away from him by herself, they were soon squashed by the difficulty of picking her way through the snow, hindered by her elaborately draped skirts. Campbell trailed them watchfully at a safe distance.

It took them ten minutes just to reach the lumber-yard that belonged to Minnie's father. Snow had built into solid drifts around the banks of lumber around the yard, but the central space was quite clear. Mr Davis had been steadily selling his planks as firewood, with more being dug out of the snow between each blizzard. A group of horses was tethered near the lumber-yard office, stamping their hoofs now and again to keep warm.

Henk Verstappen stood on the far side of the open space; his face lit up when he saw his sister and he stared at her hungrily. Three of the gunmen flanked him. Platt held Minnie Davis by one arm, his bulk dwarfing her. Her head was uncovered to the wind, a flush lending colour to her cheeks. Hugh longed to take the hood from his coat pocket and throw it to her, but kept his attention on the men.

'Let Miss Davis go,' Darrow called into the clear air. 'This is nothing to do with her. You're only building up the charges against yourself.'

Henk shook his head. 'There won't be any charges, Sheriff. Just give me Beatrix and no harm will come to Miss Davis.'

'That colourless prairie-hen,' Beatrix muttered contemptuously. Hugh increased his grip on her arm, making her squeak in pain.

'Just give it up now,' Darrow advised Henk. 'You can't get very far.'

'I'll take my chances with the blizzards,' Henk answered angrily. 'Let Beatrix go.'

Darrow spoke quietly to Beatrix. 'I'm agreeing because Minnie Davis is worth twice what you are.' He called back his answer to Henk. 'Let Miss Davis go then.'

Hugh watched Platt and released Beatrix the moment that Minnie was freed.

The women walked towards one another in the open centre of the lumber-yard. The contrast between them ran to more than Beatrix's stylish clothes against Minnie's plain, dark coat; there was a light and warmth in Minnie's plain face that rarely touched Beatrix's pretty looks. As they met, Beatrix slowed down to speak.

'Aren't you the lucky one, being rescued by your English gentleman,' she sneered.

There was open honesty in Minnie's grey-blue eyes as she answered, 'Hugh is doing his duty, as is Sheriff Darrow.'

The unashamed answer prodded at Beatrix's conscience, such as it was. Minnie Davis wasn't pretty or fascinating, but the lawmen were willing to give up their prisoner for her sake, and no one would ever spread nasty rumours about Minnie's behaviour. The knowledge made Beatrix snappy.

'Well I hope you and Hugh will be very happy together when you marry all that money of his.'

Anger flashed in Minnie's eyes, but she spoke evenly.

'We're not engaged to be married.' Her calmness in the face of insults made Beatrix even crosser.

'Is that because you don't want to marry a yellow drunk?' Beatrix said nastily.

Minnie Davis was even-tempered but she still had her limits.

'If Hugh asks me to marry him, it'll be because he loves me, not because he's trying to save me from going to jail,' she answered swiftly. 'I've never been foolish enough to murder anyone.'

'Oh!' Beatrix lost her temper completely, and flung out a wild slap.

Henk Verstappen had been watching anxiously, willing his sister to stop talking and join him. When she struck

Minnie, his own worry burst out in one reckless moment as Henk drew his Colt and fired across the lumber-yard at Darrow. Platt and the other gunmen were taken by surprise, but they reacted like the professionals they were. They fanned out as they started shooting, giving themselves room to manoeuvre and presenting a wider spread of targets for the lawmen.

15

Darrow saw the start of Henk's reckless move and acted immediately. He swung left, putting the women between himself and Henk. Even as he moved, Henk's fast shot tore through the skirt of the sheriff's coat. Darrow snapped the Winchester rifle to his shoulder, swinging it to line on McDermott as he went. He didn't know who the gunmen were but he recognized the type, and classified them as more dangerous than the angry businessman. He fired three shots at McDermott, and saw him fall.

Hugh had been watching the women and was left behind when the shooting broke out. His first instinct was to drop to one knee before reaching for his heavy Webley revolver. He immediately found himself under fire from Perry. Flurries of snow flew around the deputy as Perry's first shots ranged in on him. Hugh fired back, his concentration disturbed by a cry of pain from Minnie.

Hugh risked a quick glance at the struggling women, and got blinded by shards of ice in his face as Perry's next shot struck the frozen snow right in front of him. Unable to see, Hugh threw himself sideways and scrambled towards a fat roll of tarpaper. More bullets zinged around him. Hugh blinked and wiped his sleeve hard across his face. Ice scraped his skin, already raw from the cold air, but he could see again.

The two women were caught in the middle of the confusion. Beatrix nearly screamed with fright at the first shots, sure that someone was out for revenge on her.

'Run, Beatrix!' Henk yelled, trying to manoeuvre past his sister so he could aim at the sheriff. 'Get to the horses.'

Beatrix trusted her brother more than she trusted anyone else in the world. She grabbed up her long skirts and started to run but someone seized her from behind. Squealing in anger, Beatrix found Minnie Davis clinging to her bustle.

'Let go, you mealy-mouthed hen,' Beatrix spat, tugging at the heavy fabric. Minnie dug her heels into the snow, her eyes alight with anger. 'You're not going anywhere, you overdressed slut.'

Frustration and fury overwhelmed Beatrix.

'I am not overdressed!' she yelled. 'Let go of my bustle.' She tugged once more, but Minnie had helped around her parents' house all her life, shopping, cleaning and washing. Beatrix had never lifted heavy loads or polished a stove and she lacked the other woman's strength. Changing tactics, she lunged forward and pushed Minnie off balance. Minnie kept her grip on Beatrix's elaborate skirts, but her feet slipped and she sat down in the snow. Her grip on the bustle tightened instinctively as she struggled to keep her balance.

'Let go!' Beatrix yelled, raining wild slaps on Minnie's head and shoulders.

Henk heard Beatrix's cries and ran to her aid, as he always did. Forgetting his anger at Darrow, he ran skidding across the snow to the two women. Beatrix saw him and called for help.

'Make her let go of me, Henk. Spiteful cat!' she added to Minnie.

Minnie's head was sore from the blows but her temper was fully roused. She let go of the bustle long enough to grab Beatrix's wrist, and yanked down on her arm. Without thinking about what she was doing, Minnie bit the other woman's wrist hard enough to draw blood. Beatrix shrieked in fury and pain.

Henk arrived and picked Minnie up bodily. Minnie hung on to her grip, determined to teach Beatrix a lesson by hurting her and leaving a scar if possible. Her teeth slipped from their grip as Henk pulled her away, tearing more of Beatrix's white skin. Then Henk threw her as hard as he could.

Minnie landed in deeper snow in a tangle of skirts and petticoats. The shock of impact and the icy cold of snow driven up under her skirts took her breath away and she lay gasping.

'Henk, my hand!' Beatrix wailed, showing him the gap between her glove and her coat-sleeve, where Minnie's teeth had left red marks.

'Mamma will fix it,' Henk promised. 'Now get on a horse, quick!'

A fresh outbreak of shooting around them and a scream of agony brought Beatrix to her senses. She turned and started to run as Henk remembered his promise to get even with Sheriff Darrow.

Campbell had trailed the party from the law office to the lumber-yard. He watched from just inside the lumber-yard gates, half-hidden by a snowed-up stack of doors. As soon as the shooting broke out, his two guns slid into his hands. Campbell stalked forward, seeing Hugh coming under fire and making his frantic scramble for cover.

'That won't do ye no good,' he muttered to himself.

He was intent on his prey, raising the left Colt to aim at Hugh from behind, while keeping the other pointed roughly in Darrow's direction. The two lawmen had more than enough to occupy them; they wouldn't have time to check for an attack from behind. Campbell never thought to check his own safety.

Josh Turnage had kept out of Campbell's sight, waiting outside the lumber-yard where he could watch the short man. As soon as shooting started and Campbell began to move, Turnage thumbed back the hammers on his shotgun and followed. By the time he was inside the lumber-yard and could see Campbell, the gunman was aiming at Hugh. Turnage didn't waste time giving a warning; he simply fired from the hip. Campbell lurched forward, screaming hoarsely as the buckshot tore through him. Turnage was briefly taken aback at the amount of blood sprayed out over the white snow as Campbell fell, but he kept his head.

'Drop the guns,' he called, holding his shotgun steady.

Campbell made a feeble effort to turn, leaving bloody smears on the snow, then sagged down into stillness. The twin Colts dropped from limp fingers.

Darrow noted the bellow of the shotgun behind him and guessed what had happened without taking the time to look. His first shots had brought McDermott down, leaving him writhing on the snow with a shattered leg. Now he was after Platt, who had backed off into cover as soon as Henk started shooting.

'Give it up,' the sheriff called. 'Let Verstappen finish what he started.'

'I've been paid to do a job,' Platt called back from his place behind a tall stack of boards. The big man had heard Campbell's dying scream and knew that things weren't going well. Platt crouched slightly and started working his way to the other end of the stacked planks.

'Are you getting paid to die?' Darrow fired, hitting the top of the stack. Splinters of wood and ice sprayed out.

Platt flinched, thinking fast. He didn't want to get arrested, but the only way out of the lumber-yard was beyond the lawmen, including the one with the shotgun. He needed to even the odds a little. Platt acted as fast as he thought. He stood up where he was, using his height to get a clear shot over the stack of lumber. The sheriff twitched aside as soon as he saw the movement but Platt had been expecting that. His shot was for the one with the shotgun. He saw it hit and heard a cry of pain even as he ducked back into cover, grinning to himself.

Darrow had been surprised to see Platt stand up from behind the high cover of the planks; he hadn't realized how tall the burly man was.

'Turnage?' he called, never taking his eyes off Platt's hiding place.

'I'll live,' came the answer. There was pain in the undertaker's voice, but an undercurrent of dry humour that suggested he wasn't too badly hurt.

'Just as well,' Darrow replied, thinking about Platt and keeping half an eye on what Henk was doing over by the women. 'You wouldn't get much of a funeral, with the undertaker being dead and all.' The sheriff quickly assessed the situation.

Hugh and Perry had reached a stand-off, keeping each other occupied. Henk had dealt with Minnie and was urging his sister towards the horses. Darrow expected them to flee while they had the chance. He couldn't afford to be kept tied up with this big gunman any longer. The sheriff grabbed a stray roof-shingle that had been dropped in the snow, and hurried towards the lumber pile. The packed snow creaked treacherously under his boots, making it impossible to move silently. Darrow stopped a few paces away from Platt's hideout, breathing heavily. The clouds of icy breath around his face gave him inspiration. Darrow studied the air above the lumber pile until he saw the faint clouds of breath that told him just where Platt was hiding. The sheriff lobbed the roof-shingle over the lumber and raised his rifle almost in the same move. The shingle landed right beside Platt, startling him into jerking away and straightening up. He realized his error almost immediately and started to turn but Darrow was ready for him. As soon as Platt's head showed above the lumber, Darrow snapped off fast shots. The first tore Platt's hat off, the second ripped through his head. Platt continued turning, his body falling against the lumber before sliding down out of sight.

Perry's first shots had left Hugh at a disadvantage. The deputy's eyes were watering as he crouched in his meagre shelter, trying to get a clear shot at the other man. Perry fired rapidly, his boyish face eager as his bullets shredded the roll of tarpaper that Hugh was hiding behind. Hugh snapped off a half-aimed shot in reply, blinking the last of the snow from his eyes. Behind him came the boom of the shotgun and Campbell's dying scream. Hugh shuddered but didn't look around.

'Come out of there afore I drive you out like a scared rabbit,' Perry taunted, making a dash across the lumber-yard to get another angle on the deputy. Hugh used the brief lull to let off another shot but it went wide.

Perry laughed and fired again. The roll of tarpaper was shredded, black folds fluttering indolently in the fitful breeze.

'You're plumb running out of cover,' Perry called. He glanced about the lumber-yard, smiling as he saw Henk throw Minnie into the snow. Perry whistled when he saw Minnie's legs kicking as she struggled in the drift she'd landed in, and he made an obscene gesture.

The distraction bought Hugh enough time to act. He lay flat in the snow, staring between the torn strips of tarpaper to get a quick aim. Perry only wasted a few seconds looking at Minnie's legs but it was enough. Hugh never claimed to be any good with a gun, but when pushed he was an excellent shot. One bullet from the heavy Webley revolver tore through Perry's upper chest. The impact knocked the boyish gunman clean off his feet. Perry was dying as he hit the ground, blood filling his throat and mouth. He writhed, gasping and choking on his own blood. Hugh gulped at the sight, his imagination feeling the other man's agony and fear.

As soon as he saw Platt go down, Darrow was turning towards Henk Verstappen. He was only just in time. Henk fired off two shots, but he was no gunman and both went wide. Darrow stepped sideways as he fired in reply, and skidded suddenly on the frozen snow. His shot knocked Henk off his feet, as the sheriff too went sprawling. Both men landed hard, Henk bleeding from a shoulder wound. Darrow gasped painfully, winded by his fall.

Beatrix was untying her horse's reins when she saw her brother and the sheriff fall. She instantly saw a chance to take her revenge on the man who had stubbornly refused to do as she wanted. As always, Beatrix acted without thinking. She grabbed a rifle booted on the saddle of one of the other horses, and clumsily raised it to aim at Darrow as he struggled to get upright.

'I said you'd be sorry!' she yelled, pulling the trigger. The recoil banged the rifle butt painfully against her shoulder, but Beatrix's wild temper was up and she ignored the pain. Her shot missed, but it hit the snow encouragingly close to the winded sheriff. Beatrix yanked open the lever action and tried for a better aim.

Hugh glimpsed Darrow's fall from the corner of his eye. Forgetting about Perry, he scrambled to his feet to see if he could help. Beatrix's first shot halted him, gun in hand. He stared at her for a moment as she worked the lever action and took aim.

'Drop the gun!' he yelled, pointing the Webley at her. Beatrix didn't even look in his direction, but steadied her wavering aim. Hugh saw the wild look in her eyes, and understood that she must have looked that way when shooting Tim Judd. He gritted his teeth and fired.

Beatrix screamed as the bullet tore through skirts and petticoats to rip open her leg. She was knocked back against the horse, which saved her from falling.

'I hate you all!' she screamed, trying to aim the rifle in his direction.

She might not have hit Hugh, but he didn't want to give her the chance. Beatrix had killed Tim Judd and she'd hit Minnie. Hugh fired his last shot full into her chest.

Henk saw his sister die. He screamed irrationally, robbed of the thing he loved most in the world. Struggling to his knees, he tried to shoot the deputy. Hugh saw Henk move and fired at him, but the Webley was empty.

'Oh, hell!' Hugh ducked back into the poor shelter of the ragged tarpaper.

Oblivious of the pain in his wounded shoulder, Henk kept firing at the man who had killed Beatrix.

'Leave Beatrix alone!' he screamed mindlessly as his bullets struck closer and closer to the deputy. He didn't notice Darrow getting up and aiming his rifle. Henk never heard the sheriff's shouted warning.

Darrow saw no point in trying to reason with an armed, hysterical man. He shot to kill. Henk's pistol clicked onto an empty chamber just before Darrow's shot struck his head. Henk fell back onto the bloodied snow, just a few feet from his sister's body.

When Hugh raised his head from cover to look around, he saw Minnie kneeling by Turnage's side. The undertaker was sitting in the snow, leaning against a stack of snowy lumber. He had his hand pressed against his side, sluggish blood seeping between his fingers. Minnie was folding her muffler into a pad. Hugh told himself not to be jealous, and went to help Darrow with the sad business of clearing up.

* * *

Hugh was woken early the next morning by an exuberant kitten chasing madly around in his bedroom. It raced the length of his bed on every lap, bouncing Hugh to reluctant wakefulness as it passed. Hugh muttered a soft curse and stretched out, hearing the soft sound of water dripping somewhere. A few moments later he realized that the day was still clear, and he could see water dripping from the icicles that hung from the eaves above his window.

'It's thawing,' he told the ginger kitten.

The kitten stared back, wide-eyed. Hugh laughed and got up.

Hugh was cleaning the guns in the

office later that morning, when Darrow entered carrying several packages.

'Fried salt pork with dried apple-sauce for supper tonight,' the sheriff said with satisfaction. 'Van der Leo got back from Laramie with a sled-load of food.'

'Terrific!' Hugh picked up a tin of molasses.

'And I saw Mr Davis. He's invited us both over to share a meal with them tomorrow as a thank you for getting Minnie back safely.'

'Even better,' Hugh answered. 'Minnie and her mother are good cooks.'

'Miss Davis has a lot of good qualities,' Darrow commented.

'I know.' Hugh looked around for his box of bullets.

'Then why don't you show the good sense to ask her to marry you, and have done?'

Hugh almost dropped the box. He gave the sheriff a startled look but could read nothing from his expression.

'I . . . we . . . ' he stammered.

Darrow smiled suddenly. 'She's just the woman you need; I promise you. And I always keep my word, don't I?'

Hugh sighed. 'You do,' he agreed. 'You certainly do.'

THE END

Other titles in the
Linford Western Library:

STONE MOUNTAIN

Concho Bradley

The stage robbery had been accomplished by an old woman. Twine Fourch had never heard of a female being a highway robber before. He followed the trail all the way to a dilapidated log cabin up Stone Mountain. What happened after that no one could believe even after townsmen from Jefferson found the old log house and the skeletal dying old woman. But before the mystery could be solved there would be two unnecessary killings, a bizarre suicide and a lynching.

GUNS OF THE GAMBLER

M. Duggan

Destitute gambler Ben Crow arrives in Mallory keen to claim his inheritance, only to discover that rancher Edward Bacon has other ideas. Set up by Miss Dorothy, who had fooled him completely, Ben finds himself dangling on the end of a rope. Saved from death, Ben sets off in pursuit of Miss Dorothy, determined upon retribution. However, his quest for vengeance turns into a rescue mission when she is kidnapped by a crazy man-burning bandit.

SIDEWINDER

John Dyson

All Flynn wants is to be Marshal of Tucson, but he is framed by the territory's richest rancher, Frank Buchanan, and thrown into Yuma prison. Five years later Flynn comes out, intent on clearing his name and burning for vengeance. Fists thud, knives flash and bullets fly as he rides both sides of the law and participates in kidnapping and double-dealing. He is once again arrested for a murder of which he is innocent. Can he escape the noose a second time?